Return to Algadez

Books by Maik Nwosu

Novels
Invisible Chapters
Alpha Song
A Gecko's Farewell
The Book of Everything

Poetry
Suns of Kush
Stanzas from the Underground

Short Stories
Return to Algadez

Drama
A Quintet for Dawn

Return to Algadez
by
Maik Nwosu

CROSSROADS
New York, 2025

Published by
CROSSROADS
1178 Broadway
3rd Floor, #1333
New York, NY 10001

First paperback edition, Malthouse, 1997.
Printed in the United States of America
Cover design: Uche Ibe

ISBN 979-8-9904712-0-7

Library of Congress Control Number: 2024905760

Contents

Return to Algadez

"Dear Natasha," he began. *"Sometimes, a dream can be the peak experience in life, the channel through which our human strivings or the longings of the heart are concretized, even if ultimately into nothingness. For an addict like me stricken with the lure of the far country, the endless road where the companions of the wayfarer are the multilingual elements, it is a perennial rendezvous with the spirits of the flux, a continual return to the epiphanies of the ineffable source, especially Algadez. Yes, Algadez – both the magic of the limitless dream and an ever-expanding reality. And now that you are gone and I keep holding on to loving in the past, as the familiar song goes, I keep returning to Algadez. The journey and its penultimate conclusion grow on me, in fact, with heightening intensity."*

Setting out was simple. A jungle bag slung over one shoulder, a brave jacket and corduroys donned, the journey begins – through winding, smoke-filled paths defying temporal or geographical compartmentalization – with a voice resonant as the gurgle of a confluence town whispering insistently: "Hurry on, hurry on." Destination unknown, purpose enshrouded, my feet obey the injunction all the same. Ah, the road is life! So, on and on I traverse this universe of smoke and fauna until, past a sudden fork in the road, a quaint and moth-eaten fingerpost announces the imminence of Jerusalem. Jerusalem? I must have come a long way then – to hear cherubim sing of the mystique of the holy city or to witness heedless battles?

But when I arrive, the city is in ruins – and deserted. So the initial visual survey induces me to believe, until my eyes espy the door of a crumbling house with a mighty bell seemingly standing guard. Then, I hear raised voices from within – the same instant that I pick out the words that must have been scribbled in a hurry and with difficulty: Yom Kippur Inn. For me, it is more than a notice. It is an invitation. I walk up to the door, push the bell aside to reach the doorknob, thus causing a cavernous jangle, and become a part of the babel within.

But it is as if my entrance has not happened yet. The only member of that varied congregation who appears to have taken any notice is a portly, bearded fellow behind the bar – the innkeeper most probably. He winks at me and motions me over as if I were an old friend. I follow his signal and soon I am seated on a barstool. As soon as I am seated, he places a drink – of what? – in front of me.

"It's on the house," the innkeeper informs me in a nasal voice followed by another wink. I pick up the glass and raise it to my lips, then I hurriedly put it down again. Floating on top of the opaque liquid is the innkeeper's smiling face.

"What's the matter?" he asks with concern. "It's the best drink in the house, a special treat for wayfarers."

"I don't drink floating faces, thank you."

He looks at me strangely, then very surprisingly mutters to himself: "If I ever forget you, O Jerusalem, let my tongue cleave to the roof of my mouth."

"That's from my Warsaw chapter," he tells me. "Warsaw – where they returned hospitality with hostility. If you knew the chasms of Warsaw that I did, friend, you would understand why the Yom Kippur Inn places a high premium on hospitality – and on atonement. But I don't suppose you do. So, what's your preference?"

"Something to eat and a glass of water."

"As you wish."

To my surprise, I am served peach melba in an earthenware dish and a frosted glass of water. I eat the dessert hungrily. The taste is much better than I had expected. When I am through, the innkeeper, back from the intermittent summons of his other clients, is in front of me.

"How much?" I inquire as I lick my lips once more.

He waves aside the question as he expertly clears the dishes. *"Quem quaeritis?"* he asks me instead.

"Is that English?" I wonder.

"No, Latin," he responds with a self-congratulatory air. "It means: Whom do you seek?"

"Hurry on, hurry on," whispers the voice as if on cue.

"My quest here has just been graciously fulfilled," I tell the portly man with a hundred winks. "Now, I must be on my way. I must hurry. Thank you again for your hospitality, and please bury the ghosts of Warsaw – perhaps in the sewers of Old Jerusalem. You know what I mean?"

"Hurry? No, friend. How can I let you pass through Jerusalem without seeing the Nativity manger where the savior of the world was born? What would my defense be on the Day of Judgment? It's right here – upstairs."

Considering his claim, the somber look on his face nearly makes me hoot with laughter. But I manage to restrain myself. I confront him instead.

"You're hunting the wrong game," I say to him. "Christ was born in Bethlehem. Why do you want to distort history, or don't you know any better?"

"Of course, I do. That's why I continually strive to reconstruct a much-distorted history. The Christ we speak of – you and I – was born right here: the Christ of Jerusalem, the city of peace. How could He have been born in Bethlehem when Jerusalem, the city of God, had been chosen in the dawns before Creation as the city of eternal light? You see, mine is a superior argument, not so? For only fifty American dollars, you can rock the cradle and listen to the original Christmas carol. For a hundred, you can take pictures, and for a hundred and fifty you can make an audiovisual recording. Come on, put your money down and let's go. You will see history, like very many others before you, and your faith will move mountains. You have faith, I presume." Another wink.

Not wanting any argument with this con artist, I get up to leave. But I find that I have become a hostage, a prisoner of an undeclared war. The other patrons are all on their feet, each of them with a gun or a dagger or some other kind of weapon pointed menacingly at me. For the first time, I examine them. I marvel at Pontius Pilate washing his thickening hands in a bowl of water as if sentencing another Christ to crucifixion, at Judas Iscariot pointing a finger emitting billows of smoke at me with murder lurking in his eyes. I am astounded to witness in this same assembly Shaka the Zulu measuring my Adam's apple with an assegai and Malcom X's unmistakable intention with a rifle balanced in his hands. What logic could have brought these people together – and to protest my righteous insistence? I realize again that, here, reality itself is illogical.

The silence in the inn is deep and ominous. There is only one thing to do. I turn around to face the still-smiling innkeeper, produce a fifty-dollar bill and thrust it into his eager palms.

"Show the way," I utter.

I am led upstairs to a room where there is an empty cradle no different from those churned out regularly in furniture factories. As I stand contemplating this brazen swindle, my guide embarks on a discordant rendition of "O come, all ye faithful," one so jarringly unmelodious that I cover my ears and flee. He bounds after me and, downstairs, utters a strange farewell: "*Feliz Navidad*" – "Merry Christmas," in Spanish. I nod my head reflexively as I take my leave, with each member of that weird congregation either doffing his hat to me or according me some other form of salutation as if by succumbing to the blackmail I had become worthy of that recognition.

Even more amazing is the sight that confronts me outside the inn – the dazzle of a new Jerusalem as if risen from the ashes of history just a while ago. Where have they gone – the rubble I had seen on arrival? In place of the fallen columns are now resplendent domes proclaiming the accents of Eretz Israel. I turn back instinctively, but the inn is already lost in the mists of time, my fifty American dollars – itself of a puzzling origin – gone with it. I shake my head in deep wonder.

"I've been to Jerusalem again since you left me, Natasha. The last time I was at the inn, the old swindler took me to see not the Nativity manger but the scene of the Crucifixion, which he claimed did not happen in Golgotha but in his backyard. He even went so far to claim, with a surfeit of winks, that all the vital nodes of Christianity are in his inn. For that sight of a crooked cross with splashes of caked blood that I am almost certain he had fabricated himself, I was made to part with a hundred dollars. 'The crucifixion scene,' he told me

afterward, 'is for those in grief. You see, all grief is similar in character. They come from the death or the betrayal of the past, not so?' But how can I count you among the past when you live in my soul beyond space and time? Past they may be those supernal joys we shared, but the irony is that in writing off the past you actually redeemed it and gave it wings. Now, when loneliness haunts me like a vengeful ghost, I find that my present must continually take refuge in my past and these dimensions be necessarily fused into a whole – you, Natasha, who expanded the limits and configurations of my dream-world. But Jerusalem was only one of the milestones on the road to Algadez, on the road to you. Do you still remember Madrid – the Madrid in my dream-world sojourn to the source?"

As it happens, my next stop after Jerusalem is Madrid. This geography makes me wonder. I find myself seated by the ring, one of the spectators come to witness the confrontation between man and beast that the Spanish call *corrida de toros*. I forget about geographical truths. I am all interest, having always been fascinated by the sport without ever having had the opportunity to witness it.

I faintly decode the preliminaries incorporating an attack on the bull, with a javelin, by a man on horseback, the flowering dedication of the bull in the salt-and-pepper voice of a man not about to dare death but one set to triumph over it. Even for an amateur, I recognize the tremendous skill and daring grace with which the matador passes the bull very close to his body as if he is a god immune to injury or death. And mine is one with the reverberating cheer of the spectators. *Wallahi,* what a sight to behold! The magnificent *veronica* and the wondrous *passe natural* of the artist instill in me a sense of being a privileged spectator of a magic ring in which man, pitted essentially against himself, rises above himself. The blasts of *"Olé!"* from the excited crowd surprise me not at all.

Then, suddenly, it happens. Man and beast become one. The matador is borne on the horns of the bull and deposited at the barrier, then gored again and again. How utterly the afternoon has lost its rhyme or reason! The rescue party arrives too late. The gasp of the audience is a mighty suspension of belief: "Fernandez? Impossible!"

I am speechless.

The man beside me attracts my attention. He has his head in his hands, his deep moans somehow superimposed on the din consequent on that death in the afternoon. "Fernandez, Fernandez," he wails in a sort of funereal chant. Then he raises his head in some sort of expectation as if to assure himself it had all been a cruel joke, as if to witness once more one of Fernandez's flourishes. I grow heads, for I am at once a witness to both the impossible and the improbable, a witness to Fernandez agonizing over his own death. The man next to me is no other than the matador just dispatched by the bull to the bullfighter's city of bones.

"That Fernandez should die in the ring, but how?" he queries me agitatedly, as if I could enlighten an *aficionado* like him. "Perhaps he should die to highlight that the confrontation between man and beast is no joke at all but an art capable of high tragedy. Who else but Fernandez could have deconstructed the myth of Fernandez and, so, immortalized it?"

But I am not at all in the frame of mind – not yet, in any case – for such philosophical treatises.

"Are you not the same Fernandez who was gored just a matter of minutes ago?" I ask him the question uppermost in my mind.

"Me, Don Fernandez? You honor me, stranger. I, like many in Spain, have something of Don Fernandez in me, but there was only one Don Fernandez. There will always be. And this afternoon, you were both damned and blessed to witness the death of bullfighting. There might be a renewal. There certainly will be, but only just that. Don Fernandez was the heartbeat of the Spanish bullring."

My disbelief no less diminished, I retort: "What do you think I am – a blind idiot? You are the very same Fernandez..."

"No, no, no, senor," he cuts me off, "don't blaspheme! I am Fernandez Dias but not *Don* Fernandez Huerta. Do I look like a god, or did you think him any less?"

I study him again. Still, I am undeceived by his shabby clothes. But noting that the man is on the verge of starting a vigorous riot against me, I do not press the point. I count it as one more puzzle in the maze toward, hopefully, an impending epiphany.

"But why do they do it?" I ask instead and even manage a conciliatory smile.

"Do what?" the man hollers, rewarding me with an evil look. "Surely, this is no afternoon for half questions."

"It seems to me that there's only one way such a confrontation can end – the injury or the death of the bull or of the man. So, is it really that shocking when a bullfighter leaves the ring never to return?"

For a long while – almost too long – he studies me, apparently weighing several options. "The same tiresome old question," he says at last. "But once more, as a special tribute to Don Fernandez, the very best matador the Spanish bullring has ever produced, I'll return to the subject of the signifying metaphors of these deaths in the afternoon. I must tell you straight away that, for us *aficionados,* bullfighting is not a sport begging for justification. Yes, death comes in the ring, not as an accident, but the quintessential conclusion without which the cycle cannot be complete. But there is a similitude here to the dare of the wildlife hunter who, even with all the odds against him, stalks the animal on its own terms and in that way challenges himself. The drama of the bullring evokes the primal spirit of creation – man as the master of his own destiny, man recreating himself beyond the chapters of Genesis."

"Is that not conquistadorial?"

"Like most things in life – whether the goal be a certificate or a job or a woman's affection or the gleams of a city. Mark you, sometimes man himself is conquered. Therein lies the tragedy of the ring. But is this death, in essence, any different from the others that we resurrect from in a generation? Have you never remarked how a phase must end for a new one to begin? In the final analysis, as painful as the death of Don Fernandez is, it's not so much a loss to the ring as an enrichment. Every sport, like religion, should have its saints and martyrs and, of course, its heretics and devils. Always, life revolves between extremes."

"What about the bull?"

14

"Do you really think that the logic of the bull is different from that of man or outside that of the universe? But why is man *man* and not bull? I must go now – to pay my respects to Don Fernandez, the newest entrant to the pantheon of bullring martyrs. Sorry, stranger, I can't answer all your questions. But who can? Life is full of unanswered questions and unfulfilled answers. Only in ourselves can we find truths, our own truths. *Adios.*"

"It is intriguing, Natasha, how your searing departure seems to color every event with a different hue, sometimes even yielding a reversal of previous expositions. The night after you left me, I was once more transported to the Madrid bullring. Beside me again was no other than Fernandez – Dias? Huerta? – looking every inch alive but now the prime crusader against the sport he had once been its leading light. 'The greatest thing about bullfighting,' he lectured me, 'is also the worst thing about it – that death must come as the end. Pray, sir, where is the sense in that? If one cannot even understand the madness of men marching to short-circuit their destinies in battlefields, how then the death dance with a deliberately and systematically provoked bull? What is history but the record of endless foolishness as well as grandiose delusions? Maybe the good Lord has blessed Spain with too much sun.' That treatise accentuated for me, again, that there is always a north-end and a south-end to everything in life. For me, the north-end, so to speak, was that season of glories and dreams without any schism between us. Do you still remember the ice cream parlor where we played April and September? There are certain strings that will always bind us, always and forever, and they are neither phantoms nor strange fevers. The south-end? These days of loneliness – very much a physical pain that hurts all over, I have discovered. But, as you know, I went on, after Madrid, toward the unspoken destination. And I passed through Al-Qahirah, the land of the pharaohs."

The event I arrive just in time for is different from the brazen fraud at the Yom Kippur Inn or the afternoon highlight in the Madrid bullring. It is the marriage of Nefertiti, certainly the most beautiful woman that ever lived – and the most stylish.

"Hurry on, hurry on," *the voice whispers as if to remind me that I was not traveling entirely alone. But it is no longer the gurgle of a confluence town. It has become melodious.*

The square is awash in pomp and pageantry. On the ground is a gallery of pebbles so polished by the surf of the nearby River Nile that they gleam like sapphires. In the center of the square are two massive thrones inlaid with gleaming stones. In the taller of the two thrones sits a regal figure – a man in a saffron robe and a crown of feathers. He is ringed by attendants. In the outer ring, of which I am a part, are masses of Nilotic personages in their ceremonial dresses. I could not have looked else but out of place. As I ponder this surfeit of resplendence, thick volumes of mist rise from the shimmering surface of the Nile and imbue the entire scene with a foggy incandescence.

"There sits Ikhnaton," *the unusually loquacious voice answers my thoughts. "Akhenaten, son of Amenhotep III, husband of Nefertiti."*

The last bit makes me wonder at its sense of historical progression. Before I can voice that feeling, however, I feel the outer ring shiver with excitement as the rattle of hooves announces the arrival of a long line of picturesque chariots.

The chariots draw to a stop at the edge of the ring, and the gates of the Nile are thrown open. I witness the naiads of the deep ascend to the earth, costumed and equipped as minstrels. The music that now wafts through the air enkindles an elliptical oscillation of virtually everything. Is this still Egypt or the gateway to the fabled paradise?

As one, the naiads glide up to the column of chariots. The doors are opened and out steps colorful priest-like figures. Even among this blindingly colorful group, one figure stands out. She has, for a headgear, a rainbow of seashells; for earrings, kaleidoscopic emeralds. Her silken dress clothes a luscious frame. And on her feet are furry sandals. Around her, as her retinue now oscillates toward Akhenaten, are four figures clad in ethereal white robes with orbs of frankincense which they swing to and fro, further enriching the already coated air with the scents of emperors and gods.

"And here now is Nefertiti," *the voice whispers again. "Nefertiti,*

aunt of Tutankhamun."

Akhenaten now rises, as if he were the Great Pyramids come to life. Accompanied by his own train, he proceeds in measured movements to the epicenter of the square where I notice, for the first time, a tripod of fire. Each train comes to a stop a few steps from the tripod. The music stops. The chief priest – so I dub the incense-bearer in front of Nefertiti – raises his face to the sun and begins, from the deepest recesses of his priestly being, a deep chant in the language of the Nile. All around me, everyone – except the priests, the celebrants, and the naiads – prostrate to the earth. I am too lost in reverence for promptness. A hand, frail and scratchy, grips my ankles in an apparent bid to bring me down to earth, even as the voice whispers: *"Down, down."* But the painful scratch drives me, reflexively, to stamp the frail hands. A sharp cry rings out. The chief priest stops in mid-trajectory, turns, and beckons to me.

"Hurry on, hurry on," the voice resumes its signature chant. I wonder, not for the first time, at its meaning and timing.

I am propelled to the inner ring by a force beyond myself.

"Behold, he of whom the oracles spoke," the chief priest announces to the gathering, "the messenger of Amon-Ra, chief of the deities. What messages do you bring to the royal solemnization of love and all things bright and beautiful?"

"Greetings," I hear myself utter.

At this, a great cry rises again from the outer ring. Both Akhenaten and Nefertiti accord me salutations. I grow heads.

"Time now for the bridal toast," announces the priest.

"The gates of Tutankhamun: the gates of Egypt. The fires of Akhenaten: the fires of Al Qahirah. The tones of the Nile: the tones of the world."

"Tutankhamun" before Tutankhamun?

The chief priest now dips a finger in the tripod, consecrates the foreheads of the bride and the bridegroom, apparently says a prayer in what I suppose must be the lost language of the enlightenment, and declares the marriage accomplished. For a moment, there is a great stillness, then as the couple are firmly clasped in each other's embrace, a jubilant pandemonium erupts. I find myself borne high on anonymous shoulders and passed on and on, alarmingly toward the shimmering Nile.

"That was the first time, Natasha, the magic synthesis of the bright and beautiful that I experienced in Egypt en route to Algadez – to you. I was to wonder intensely about the lifespan of the bright and beautiful in my subsequent stopover in the land of the pharaohs after you unilaterally upset the state of our union. On that voyage, I witnessed, to my utmost chagrin, the marriage of a haggard Nefertiti with a skull for a head and a hunchbacked Akhenaten. From the depths of the muddy Nile emerged not a choir of naiads but pyramid tombs out of which spewed forth the mummies of Egyptian princes and kings. And when it was time for the bridal toast, the skull underscored this reversal. 'The tomb of Akhenaten: the tomb of Egypt. The ashes of Akhenaten: the ashes of humankind. The chasms of the Nile: the chasms of the world.' Is it that when you separated yourself from our union, Natasha, the light went with you and I have been walking in the shadow of the valley of death, overwhelmed by the darkness of solitude and absence, ever since?

"But Egypt was not the journey's end. Algadez was – Algadez, the source where the springs of our fountain first sprouted and our immersion began; Algadez, where I was born anew; Algadez, the briefest but the longest."

After Egypt, I find myself transported into the clouds. For a while, I am blinded by blue mists. When my eyes grow accustomed to this environment, I discover that I am in the center of a flamboyant garden stretching in four directions. And I can hear the music of the spheres, which humbles the skill of the naiads, seeping from every pore in this universe. The atmosphere, at once ethereal and soporific, with myself alone at the center, makes me wonder: Is this another Eden?

As if in answer, an eclipse blots out the flood of light. From this fabulous darkness emerges a dazzling figure of light that once more restores the sun. I am forced to my knees by the transcendental beauty of this epiphany.

"Here now the answer to your prayers."

There is a question – is there? – in the voice. I nod my head vigorously and kiss the earth with my forehead to indicate my complete satisfaction. When I raise my head, the figure of light is kneeling opposite me with a flower which she now extends to me. I accept the offer, make a wish – "That we may be one" – and plant it at the crossroads.

"Who are you?" I inquire in an unsteady voice.

She puts a finger across my lips instead and whispers with the voice of the evening breeze: "Algadez. Here is what matters now."

Algadez? Is here then the Algadez that had been variously forecast for me, where I am to be filled with new life – the source, the dream? Algadez!

"Algadez – the great conclusion?"

"The journeys of life go on and on."

"But surely we will transcend this dream, transform it into reality?"

"Where does the dream end and life begin?"

I am once more struck speechless by her overwhelming magnetism, but I sense that time is running out. "We must transcend this dream!"

"Our dreams become us, still the gates of dream are taller and wider than those of the world."

"I've descended valleys, scaled mountains, done a thousand spins – in order to meet you. I want you, Algadez!"

Without a word, she puts her hand on my forehead and sprinkles sand around the flower I had planted. "The dream is true," I hear her intone. As the last grain of sand trickles out of her hands, the eclipse descends once more. I instinctively sense what will happen, but I lunge after her into the fabulous darkness too late.

"As you know, Natasha, that lunge earned me a collision with my bedroom wall and for a couple of days I walked around with a swollen forehead. And exactly one week later, when I was already tottering on the verge of lunacy, I met you – the Algadez of my dreams – in the last coach, after I had walked through the train looking for an empty seat. I found that seat beside you and I knew that the dream,

indeed, was true, that the journey through Jerusalem, Madrid, Al-Qahirah – the revelation of the tones of the world in three significant phases – was a variegated preamble with an elevating purpose. For what would my life have been without you? In you, Natasha, I found that soulmate that I had feared I would never find. When we became one, I achieved a rare harmony with the rhythm of the universe, which is why your departure, your taciturn goodbye note, both puzzles and fragments me. I am fast losing any claim to harmony or balance. Is the world around me taking on a different character or is my imagination, diseased by your absence, peopling the universe with the forces of my own destruction?

"The dream is no longer true. When I returned to Algadez last night, I was astounded by the sight and sound of dying birds, decaying flowers, and funeral drums. At the crossroads where we had planted the flower of our spring was a huge mound with a solitary wreath. Death in the garden of life? As I stood contemplating that mound, I felt a thunderous vibration and saw the earth open up in huge cracks as if to regurgitate the dead. But the grave was empty. So, where then are you, Natasha? Will this letter even get to you? Is your old family address still true? Is anything still true? If you do receive this letter, this is a passionate appeal from a dying heart for that breath of life which only you can infuse in me. If I had made the journey myself, I would be struck dumb in your presence, as often happens, by your magnetism. But I will surely make that journey if I have to. Do, please, come back to me, dear heart.

"I have not lost faith. I cannot. And I will not. 'It is finished,' the voice harshly announced to me when the earth opened up on my return to Algadez. But how can it be finished, ever, when you still live in my heart – beyond space, beyond time – in that magical consciousness alive with endless possibilities and imminent probabilities. Forever and forever, Natasha, the two of us."

—

1993

The Sakpoba Mermaid

He stood by the side of the road filled with an apprehension rooted in the stories he had heard about the city. Not that he was new to cities. After all, was he not resident in Lagos, the country's bustling business capital? But Benin was notorious for its multiple-headed terrors. His friends had warned him that only two types of people visited the city these days – fools and criminals. Yet there he was at the corner of Third East Circular waiting for a taxi.

He had arrived in Benin that Friday for a surprise weekend visit only to learn that his would-be host had traveled to Lagos to visit his family and would not be back until Monday. Still bent on exploring the city, he then faced a problem he had not reckoned with – accommodation for the next three days. But he was not much perturbed because he had money to spend.

"Taxi, drop!" he hailed a cab.

"Where to?" the driver inquired.

"Just drive around. I want to see the city," he said when he had settled into the backseat, his bag carefully placed on his lap.

"Na twenty naira per hour-o," the driver informed him.

Because he did not want to give the heavyset driver the impression that he had a lot of money on him, he began to haggle over the price.

"All right," he agreed, after he felt he had created the picture he wanted in the driver's mind. "Twenty naira per hour, so be it."

For more than an hour, he was driven all over the town and shown important places. There was a quaint beauty about the cramped, graying town that intrigued him. One moment, he felt he was face to face with the past – the days of Mother Emotan or General Ebokinwin or Oba Esigie. The next moment, he was confronted by evidence of modernity. Before the expiration of an hour, he had found ample reasons to like the town. Only a few doubts still remained: What about those stories about young men who walked the streets with trouble-hunting daggers and pistols in their pockets? What about the tales about young women who walked about with trouble-ready shorts underneath their skirts? One of his friends had even dubbed the town "the city of blood." And he had no liking for blood, absolutely none.

"Do you know a small, inexpensive hotel where I can sleep?" he asked the cabdriver.

"Dey full everywhere."

"Fine. Take me to the best one. But, first, where can I pick up a woman for the night?"

"Ah, dat na small tin'," the man said with a laugh. "No be Benin we dey? Make we go Ring Road."

Ring Road that night was like a military parade ground, the paraders in this case being streetwalkers whose parades were however bereft of any military discipline. He did not really want a mercenary from a military parade ground in a town where he was scared of everybody. But he saw no way he could get any self-respecting stranger into his bed that night. So, he beckoned to one of the women that struck his fancy.

Although she could not be described as pretty, she radiated a compelling sex appeal. Her face made him think of a hastily carved Christmas mask, her robust frame of the fattening room, her dress of prettified mannequins. Studying her, he felt that he could outfight or outrun her if need be.

Getting her into the taxi took only a few words. But she would not go with him to his intended hotel room.

"I have to pick up something from my house," she insisted, her smoky voice not failing to make an impression on him.

"It'll take no time at all. Are you scared of going to my house?" she asked, correctly deciphering his fear.

"Scared? Why should I be?" he said with a boldness that he did not feel. Fear, however, had never been able to stop him from being his adventurous self.

"Do you know Sakpoba Lane?" she asked the driver.

"Nowhere wey I no sabi for Benin," the man declared importantly.

"That's my street."

"Oga, we go reach der?" The driver sought confirmation from his principal passenger.

"Well, let's make the damsel happy so that she'll do what is right before God and man."

A packet of cigarettes and a lighter appeared in her hands as the car moved off. Soon, they all – the driver and his two passengers – had a cigarette between their fingers.

"My name is Cynthia," she told him.

"Mine is Uzoka."

The moment the taxi turned into Sakpoba Lane, Uzoka lost interest in Cynthia's seductive appeal. Sakpoba Lane was one of those dingy streets where aging men, exhausted and frustrated, regularly sat in front of grumbling houses in the evenings and hurled sultry monologues at the sky. It was one of those backstreets in the anciently modern city where native doctors played gods with their magic tom-toms in the silence of deep nights. So the cabdriver humorously remarked. Each of his observations only heightened Uzoka's fear, but he was careful not to give his feelings away.

Following Cynthia's direction, the driver pulled up in front of an unnumbered house – a freshly painted bungalow that sat on a large piece of land like a sated toad and was partially hidden by a shrub. There was no one about, and the windows and the entrance door were all shuttered.

"Won't you come in?" Cynthia invited Uzoka as she got out of the car.

"No, I'll wait here. Don't be long."

She smiled. "Come on, don't be such a coward. The house is all mine and you've got nothing to fear from me, absolutely nothing."

"I'm not afraid. But I prefer to wait here."

"To tell the truth, there's something I want to show you."

"In the house?" Uzoka asked, regarding the brooding being with disfavor.

"In my house, yes."

"What's that?"

"My slaughter slabs," she replied with a throaty laugh. "Oh, come on. Since you've come this far, what are a few more steps? I never go out with any man who's afraid of stepping into my house. It means you're scared of me, and fear is a negative feeling."

"You're a nagger, aren't you? OK, let's go."

To take the decision was one thing, to actualize it another. Dare he leave his bag in the car even for a few minutes? Again, Cynthia correctly placed her finger on his dilemma. She leaned across the window and lifted the bag as if it were much lighter than it actually was.

"I'll take care of the bag," she said. "I can see you don't want to be parted from it. What are you – a traveling salesman?"

"Traveling salesman? The ideas you get! I'm a business executive."

"Who is not?"

Uzoka, a freshly employed graduate on his first leave, had not intended to describe himself as he had just done, but it had needed only such a quip as Cynthia's to provoke his Lagos tongue. But now that he had hung his nonexistent banner in the four corners of the globe, he had no intention of retracting his story. After all, he reasoned, exaggeration could also be an effective protection mechanism.

Having unlocked the entrance door, Cynthia ushered him into her bedroom. "This is where I was born," she said, sitting beside him on the couch, "and probably where I will die."

"Who else lives here?"

"No one. I'm all alone."

"What about your family?"

"What are you – a policeman? Well, the house belonged to my parents, but they're both dead. And I'm an only child."

This answer did not reassure Uzoka. Instead, it made him even more uneasy. He remembered the stories he had heard about men who had picked up strange women only to ultimately – and sometimes fatally – discover that they were spirits. Had she not already given him enough reason to suspect she was an extraordinary being? How else could he explain her aura of virgin-like innocence and her mind-deciphering ability? And there was an eerie atmosphere in the house, reinforced by the cover-all shadows in the poorly lit street and bedroom. Was she real? Was the house real? He was not sure. But he was in no hurry to save himself from the danger he believed he could sense. He was like a moth, she a bright light. There was something about her, a mystifying magnetic power that overpowered his urge to get up and bolt away but instead held him captive beside her.

She put on an audio cassette and the room was filled with Afrobeat music. She got up and began to dance. He kept his eyes on her hips, hypnotized. There was something about the way she moved that resurrected the scenario of the midnight dance of mermaids he had experienced in several dream-worlds. She stopped when the music stopped.

"Do you like my dancing?" she asked.

The question broke the spell.

"Yeah. But isn't it time we got going?"

"Where're you staying?"

"I've not checked into any hotel yet."

"In that case, don't. Let's spend the weekend together right here."

"Thanks for the offer, but I'd rather stay in a hotel..."

"Come on, do you think it's every man who winks at me that I invite to my house?"

"But we don't know each other. How do you know I'll not strangle you in the night?"

She laughed. "You won't. No strangler can withstand the forces in this house."

"What forces?"

"Those of my trinity."

He thought it best not to prolong the talk. "Thank you all the same but..."

"You're my guest," she said firmly, "and I won't take 'no' for an answer. I never sleep in strange hotel rooms anyway. What do you think I am – a street-corner prostitute? So it seems, probably, but that's not what I am. Which hotel do you think will cuddle you as I will? Or is my house not good enough for his international excellency?"

"Not that."

"You're still scared of me?"

"Not at all."

Now on the defensive, he was soon conquered. "All right, all right," he said in the end, "but we have to go back to town with the cabdriver. I want to leave my mark in one or two spots in this city tonight."

"Sure."

Driven in the same cab they had come with, they returned to the city center. From one beer parlor to another they went until they were both tipsy. Only then were they driven back to her house and they staggered off to bed – but not until the driver had extracted his fare from Cynthia, who had confounded the stranger from Lagos by insisting on footing every bill.

Later, the midnight throbbing of tom-toms in Cynthia's backyard whipped Uzoka awake. His heartbeat immediately became the frenzied pounding of intoxicated drums. So great was his apprehension. Was he to end up as the victim of a ritual murder? Were all his lofty dreams to be thus rudely terminated? Why had he been so reckless in a city that everyone had warned him was the happy hunting ground of armed bandits and vampires? The rush of self-blame compounded the dizziness induced by his wild fright.

"Have no fear," Cynthia whispered in his ear, placing a hand on his chest. "So far as I'm with you, nothing will happen to you."

Her reassurances calmed him somewhat. "Why this midnight tom-tom?" he asked.

"It's my uncle," she whispered. "He's a native doctor, and he conducts midnight rituals for some of his clients."

"Are you also a native doctor?"

"Oh no," she replied with a laugh, then she lit two cigarettes – one for him, one for her.

The throbbing of the tom-toms was now complemented by the jangling of anklets and the chants of a spectrum of voices led by a cracked, male voice he suspected was the native doctor's. Caught between his fear and her reassurances, he knew the tom-toms had banished sleep from his eyelids that night. Her reassurances? Did he even know who she really was that he should feel reassured by her, by her probably false words?

"Now awakened, my tummy reminds me we ate nothing last night, only beer and cigarettes," her voice obstructed the train of his thoughts. "I'm sure you must be hungry too, so I'll blend something."

"Now?"

"Why not? It's my house. Be good enough to come along and give me a hand, p-l-e-a-s-e."

She swung out of bed and switched on the colored light bulb. Stark naked, she left the bedroom. He dashed after her, equally naked. So great was his fear of remaining in the room alone. Had she not reassured him that nothing would happen to him as long as she was with him? Had he any alternative than to believe her?

Through a crack in the kitchen door, he watched weird figures dancing around a pot of fire.

"Don't!" Cynthia whispered fiercely over her shoulders.

His response was instant obedience. But how had she – with her back turned – known what he was doing? Had she other eyes than the frontal two visible to him? He suffered another wave of self-blame. Why had he challenged his guardian spirit to a wrestling contest? What would be the tragic conclusion of his misadventure?

"Come and give me a hand," Cynthia, who was seated on a kitchen stool in front of a gas cooker and a kitchen cabinet, called out.

"Too many cooks spoil the broth," he replied mechanically.

"I don't just cook," she told him, "I b-l-e-n-d. Be a darling and give me a hand."

For the next half-hour or so, he helped out as she wanted – until she finished her blending.

The tom-toms and the dancing suddenly ceased. The cracked voice embarked on an interminable chant or monologue in a language that Uzoka did not understand. Cynthia rose from her stool at about the same time and came toward him. She put her arms around him and drew him to her.

"I love you," she whispered in his ear.

Despite his unease, his manhood stiffened, provoked by the physical contact with her naked body.

"See, see," she teased him. "A man is a man is a man, fear notwithstanding."

He smiled, then covered her questing nipples with his passionate mouth.

"We're in the kitchen, remember? Come on, let me prove my love to you."

Her meaning was different from his understanding because, instead of her bedroom, she ushered him into a different room. In this well-maintained room was a monstrous tombstone. The epitaph was a single word: *Mama.* As Uzoka stood there bewildered, the tom-toms and the jangling anklets and the voices began making their representations once more.

"What's the matter, my dear?" Cynthia wondered, once more placing her magical hand on his chest.

"Is-is this re-al?" a confused Uzoka wanted to know.

"Of course. This is my mother's grave. She was born in this room. She died in this room. So, I buried her here. That way, we're still together. And will always be. I consult her from time to time."

"You what?"

"In difficult times, I seek her advice. Well, not hers alone. Come on."

In an adjoining room was her father's tombstone – almost an exact replica of her mother's, except for the epitaph: *Papa.*

"He was not born in this room, but here he died," she explained. "On the same day as my mother. They had had a terrible quarrel, apparently the first serious quarrel since their decades-old marriage. My mother committed suicide. She started her journey only about an hour earlier than my father."

"Why do you brutalize me so, Cynthia, if – as you said just a short while ago – you love me?" Uzoka pleaded with tears in his eyes and in his voice.

"You don't understand. You're the seventh pair of eyes that have seen the inside of these rooms since after the funeral. What girl would introduce a man she didn't love to her parents?"

"Do you have beer in the house?" he pleaded.

"Come on, let's eat first, then lots of beer and cigarettes and lots of *smooching*, eh?"

"Forget about everything else, p-l-e-a-s-e. I just want to get drunk."

"Whatever you say, my midnight husband."

Within him, Uzoka began a passionate prayer to a God he had largely disregarded for the peaceful repose of his soul, certain then that he would not leave that house alive. What else could his hostess be but an unreal entity who apparently entertained, tormented, then sucked dead fools like him from time to time? Nevertheless, it was with relative equanimity that he raised the first bottle of beer – poisoned? – to his lips, the calm that sometimes comes from resignation. The pity, he lamented in his heart, was that no one would ever find his corpse.

When the stranger from Lagos, to his utmost amazement and despite his nightmares, found himself still alive the next morning, he announced to his host that he had to return to Lagos that day to attend to certain pressing engagements.

"Don't go – yet," Cynthia pleaded. "I know how you feel, but there's absolutely nothing to fear from me or from my house. I swear. Let's spend the weekend together right here. Two more days. My family has a deep-rooted tradition of hospitality that is often quite baffling to strangers. Not like certain people who, because they're criminals and witches, view everyone with suspicion. You see, *though we travel the world over to find the beautiful, we must carry it with us or find it not.*"

"Where did you learn to quote Emerson?" Uzoka could not contain himself. "Who are you, Cynthia?"

Cynthia laughed. "Don't even attempt to understand me," she said. "How can anyone reconcile the several selves that is Cynthia? But never believe that the oasis is the desert because it fraternizes with the desert. Just let our masks be and let us remain what we already are – the dust-stranger and the maiden of an ancestral river."

Within him, Uzoka began another passionate prayer.

Uzoka did not leave that day – or the day after. And apart from some disturbing indicators that all was not what it was or should be, he did not regret not leaving. He soon discovered that he and his host had several things in common.

Cynthia's ability as a blender was out of this world. In the kitchen she would become a kitchen magician, just as she became a sex magician in bed or a dance magician in her bedroom and everywhere else. She did with few condiments what he doubted that any chef could do with much more, and she introduced him to new culinary delights.

"Now, I believe that by special arrangement the devil can see God," he said after an exceedingly delicious lunch.

Cynthia exploded into one of her tonal laughters. "See, you've even begun to speak with the tongue of our Delta."

Uzoka wanted to explore the town some more, but Cynthia did not want to leave the house.

"You want to satisfy your prime reason for coming to Benin?" she said. "What more do you want to explore? I am Benin."

"Not again, Cynthia, please."

"In any case, this is the perfect weekend – two lovers alone in a capsule of a hundred pleasures."

"What sort of lovers are we when you don't even know or want to know who I am?"

"Do you believe that? I know who you are. I came to Ring Road to meet you. Why do you think I procured in advance everything we'll need for a pleasurable weekend together? You didn't tell me your preferences, did you?"

"Cynthia, p-l-e-a-s-e."

"All right, all right."

Monday morning made an instant enemy of Uzoka – for dawning. He no longer wanted to leave Cynthia and the pleasures she was capable of conjuring. He no longer cared if she was a ghost or a demon. In just three days, she had given him more pleasure than he had ever had at any time in all his twenty-five years. And she had not let him spend even a kobo. To think that he had been warned not to visit Benin City! *The city of blood?* What a fable!

"You and I forever, eh?" Cynthia read his mind. "No, my dear. It can't be. See, all the cigarettes and beer and foodstuff are finished. We were meant to be together for three days only."

"Some other time then, eh?"

"Only three days were meant..."

"By whom?"

"You still want to unmask me?" she asked with characteristic laughter.

"Please, Cynthia, give me a hint at least of who you are."

"I'm not that much of a puzzle once you cease to be an astrologer who studies the moon as the sun because the sun is the moon. And why do you want to trouble yourself with the reconciliation of shades of meaning that should be left in their different dimensions? As you can never quite comprehend the mysteries of Benin so can you never quite understand me."

"Well, whatever is or will be, I'll never forget you, Cynthia. Let me at least pay you for the three days. I have enough money..."

"To pay for what – the food or the beer or the tom-tom beats or my body or what? Don't worry. Our bills follow us wherever we go until they're paid. You're a bill that I once neglected."

"What are you talking about?"

"I have given you a glimpse into the mind of the universe. And that's why you were drawn to Benin – by the strings of your own destiny. But do not exert yourself unduly, my dear. Do think of me sometimes and wish me well. I'll do the same for you. Now, come let us kiss and part, stranger."

When he eventually left the house, Uzoka did not know whether to believe it was indeed Monday morning or still Friday evening. The farther away he moved from her house, the more those three days seemed like a dream.

—

1990

The Gray Hairs of Gafaru

The room had what he called "a Dickensian appearance." Its dust and cobwebs were reminiscent of those that had marked forever the hour of Miss Havisham's aborted great expectations. The reason for the state of Etiebet's room however was not only a feeling of being rejected but also that of rejecting – and discarding. So there were piles of discarded garments, books, currency notes, pictures, and all sorts of things all over the one-bedroom apartment. There was only a little free space left in the living room, where Etiebet, who had finally rejected his bedroom, now slept. The rejected bedroom had become one massive dump in which Okonkwo stammered at Raskolnikov and Armstrong trumpeted to Watanabe in discarded tomes – with rats and cockroaches, thus convoked, as the lords of the piles.

The kitchen was about the only other room in the house which had a semblance of functionality, for although Etiebet had rejected several kinds of food, he was yet to reject the necessity of eating. Once, he had attempted to but had been forced, after a few days, to rub off the crossbones he had painted on the kitchen door and put it to use once more. He considered his own cooking a preferable alternative to the overpriced concoctions available in the bukaterias around his house. Occasionally, the master of the house would reject the piles and clear them off in a sudden, desperate burst of energy, but they always returned. In between Etiebet's cycles of passion was a long span occupied by a lull of passivity during which period he sometimes rejected even the very act of rejecting itself.

The moments he cared to go back in time, Etiebet could somewhat locate how it had all started. In those heady days when the whole world – its circumference of pleasure and communion – had been his playground, he had come close to sealing the bond he had thought existed between him and Lola. At their regular table in Simi's Café, he had finally proposed to her. It was the seventh anniversary of their relationship. After a lavish meal came his chosen moment. He felt like a speech.

"One last toast, Lola," he proposed. "To us, to our tomorrows – those happy days thereafter when we will always be together, the center of one happy family. I'm asking you to marry me, my dear."

She clinked her glass with his, rather too calmly, sipped her drink – rather contemplatively – and did nothing more. Could it be that he had overwhelmed her into speechlessness? No, she did not look overwhelmed.

"What's the matter, Lola? I'm asking you to marry me."

"I know," she said as she finally put down her glass. "I heard you."

Her disappointing flatness of tone seemed to him especially rehearsed to wreck the magic of the moment. He did not know what exactly he had expected but certainly not that tone. What had he not seen, even with his eyes open, all these years? What had he not heard?

"Say something, Lola. Say something *positive* before I die."

She managed a smile. "I'll have to think about it."

"Think about what? What are you going to think about that you haven't thought about all these years? The proposal, I had thought, was more or less a formality. Or did I do it the wrong way?"

"Not really, ET. But, you know, no woman is ever sure about these things until she is sure."

"Fine, then say 'yes' and dispel your doubt. After all the years we've been together, we're practically married anyway."

"It's not the same thing."

He knew the magic was gone, the night ruined, but he managed to mumble his way through. When he finally dropped her off at her apartment, he did ask: "So, how long is this great thinking process going to take?"

"I really have to think everything through, then I'll call you. Do try and understand, ET. It's best that I'm sure."

"I understand nothing. You know that."

Nothing went right after that. The invitation came two weeks later requesting his presence at the marriage of Lola, his intended, and Frank, his best friend. Its arrival served to explain, to him, why his attempts to get in touch with Frank lately had been subtly but unusually rebuffed.

The next day, alone at their old haunt, Simi easily got the story out of him.

"So, Lola runs off with Frank and you feel the world must come to an end, with a large measure of prompting from yourself?" Simi was moved to say to him. "Why have you apparently convinced yourself that you must cease to function because of Lola and Frank? Listen to me: I am a citizen of this wide, wild world full of demons and angels. Every day and night, right here in this café, I travel hundreds, sometimes thousands, of miles in several directions. Life is simply what you go on and on with until you lose it. Because you stop won't make it stop or even slow down, sometimes. The streets of the world teem daily with men and women disappointed in love. Are you any greater or less than the rest of the world? Is love, that great romantic fable, any greater or any less?"

"You don't understand."

"I do, believe me. I've also had the same experience."

"No two experiences are the same, Simi. Each one involves different people and various responses. If Lola had only walked out on me, the story would have been different – regardless of our long relationship and mutual promises of eternity. But to get married to Frank, that's the dirty and the most hurtful part. It means they've probably been having an affair while pretending loyalty to me. How will I ever believe in friendship after this? And what would life be without such beliefs? I appreciate your concern, but don't try to powder the ugly face of tragedy."

"Tragedy? Oh, come on. What then will you call the mass carnage around the world? Come on, you have to thank God for little mercies, not that I believe they are 'little.'"

"Personal tragedies sometimes outweigh the distant tragedies of the world, at least in the hearts of the victims. There is the tragedy which makes you call on God to remake the world, and there is the tragedy that tasks your belief in God. Mine wrenches at the very core of my being and it blots out the beauty of the universe. Love is the center of the world. If you've loved, Simi, truly loved, you'll know that to lose that is to lose a deep part of yourself. To add to that loss a stab in the back is to have one's experience exemplify the degradation of humanity. Seven is the sign of victory, Simi. What did I do to deserve this fate after seven years with Lola?"

"This is not the time for self-pity, man. You're being intellectual, as usual. I'm also interested in philosophy, as you very well know. But what if you've studied the Kabala, magic, the mystic aura? I've always said that the more a man knows the more he feels. This is the time to get out into the open country and let the wind blow in your hair and the waves pound in your ears. You'll discover that, despite all the heartaches, it's still a good life. You're neither the first nor the last of the beautiful ones. Even if no one else does, you should give yourself all the love you deserve, ET."

"ET. Jesus! She still called me that even on that night. Can you imagine that? That's beautiful, isn't it? ET – Etiebet? Extra Terrestrial? Extra Soft? I must have been extra soft in the head these past seven years. Why is love so very mysterious and demanding?"

He was the last customer to leave Simi's that night. And he left in an unusual state of drunkenness. It was the last night he ever drank beer, the last time he ever went to Simi's Café. Get out into the open country and let the wind blow in his hair, Simi had counseled. What poetic nonsense! The wind, dry and portentous, was already blowing inside his head. It was easy to gloss over love if it had never dug its clasping roots into one.

Simi's Café was the first in a long list of rejections that followed. Next came the relegation of all the memorabilia associated with Lola into forgotten corners. The turn of the books arrived the day he reread Helen of Troy's argument in what used to be one of his favorite books: "*It's the illusion you fall in love with. And no matter how often it occurs, no matter how wise you are as to what the end will be, one more illusion is welcome – for only while it lasts do we catch a vision of our best selves. In that sense, love is a disease, and incurable.*" The rejections continued until the logic and the act became blurred and he was both lost and self-trapped in a state of rejecting and discarding.

On this morning, he woke up with the firm decision to do away with everything altogether. He would go to Gafaru in an attempt to fathom the mind of the universe and perhaps discover peace again. G-a-f-a-r-u – the place once described by Frank as "the mountains of renewal." In those heady days, they had gotten into one of their familiar arguments. An inebriated Frank had suddenly begun to recite: "*On came the crushing, rolling noise, and the sound of it was as the sound of a forest being swept flat by a mighty wind, to be tossed up again like so much grass, and hurled in thunder down a mountainside. Nearer and nearer it approached; now flashes of light, forerunners of the revolving pillar of flame were passing like arrows through the rosy air; and now the edge of the pillar itself appeared. Ayesha turned towards it, and stretched out her arms to greet it. On it rolled very slowly and lapped her round with fire. I saw the essence run up her form. I saw her lift it with both hands as though it were water, and pour it over his head. I even saw her open her mouth and draw it down into her lungs, and it was a dread and wonderful sight.*"

"The spirit of Life. Only a fantasist like H. Rider Haggard could have created that 'dread and wonderful sight,'" Etiebet had said.

"You think so? The fantastic isn't always far away. There's this place called Gafaru near my hometown. The name means 'the mountains of renewal.'"

"Real mountains?"

"Well, three hills, but that's hardly the point. It's the habitation of gray-haired old men filled with the knowledge of the universe and who renew the spirit of life in the needy. It reminds me very much of Haggard's lost city of Kor."

"Have you been to this Gafaru?"

"So many years ago, as a kid growing up in the open country. But I know some fellows who've gone on my advice. I'm told the place hasn't changed."

"And were their pilgrimages rewarded?"

"The magic of Gafaru never fails. Someday, I plan to write about the place – to remind us that the answers to our quests may lie in our history, in alternative forms of reality. '*How but in custom and in ceremony are innocence and beauty born?*'"

"So your Gafaru is the new Byzantium, no country for old men but of '*sages standing in God's holy fire?*' I, too, can quote Yeats."

"I know. But everything in Yeats and Haggard and the rest of them are right here – in our folk traditions. And, I tell you, Gafaru is the key."

"Is any one place, any one event, that?"

"One day, we'll find out, ET. Together."

One day. Words now lost to treachery.

Etiebet reckoned the time had come for him to find out for himself. It was ironic that Lola – Lola and Frank, rather – had served as the key. G-a-f-a-r-u. The name had a certain ring. Maybe that was what Simi had meant, unwittingly, by advising him to get out into the open country and let the wind blow in his hair.

"Today, I leave for Gafaru," he wrote to Lola the morning he left. "Frank called the place the mountains of renewal. I mean to find out. Not if our love can be renewed. Incredible as it sounds, I still love you. But I'm not sure I want you back. The sort of love I believed we shared is lost in the mists of time. I mean to find out the logic of the universe – the logic behind the tragedies of being, such as your betrayal. I mean to find answers to questions that defy even formulation. I mean to find peace or harmony with the cosmic whole. I understand that the magic of Gafaru never fails. I now know how much of a scoundrel Frank is, but I've not lost my belief in his knowledge of these things. One day, you too will also have to set out for Gafaru, wherever your own mountains of renewal may be. May your road also be rough." To think that he used to tell her teasingly: "Your love will always bring you back to me." Ah, this life!

He posted the letter on his way to the train station. Then he took the long-distance train to Somorika, the railway station nearest to Gafaru. He managed to sleep a little but, mostly, he kept awake all through the night, his mind a cinematic reel of montages from the past. It was an indulgence he had rejected in the past three weeks since the Café Wall as he had come to dub Lola's rejection of his proposal. Sifting the past very carefully, he could identify the telltale signals that should have warned him that her affection toward him was cooling off. And what about all those *innocent* words and acts of affection between her and Frank? The more he thought about these things, the more he realized that he was one of those people who were so hypersensitive that it was difficult for them to recover from such a betrayal. Lola was the past, yet Lola was still the present. He was going in search of the future. He had once told her: "You're forever." He was going in search of the end of forever.

The train pulled into the station at dawn. It was a small station. And a small town. S-o-m-o-r-i-k-a. The name conjured up a certain image. The image and the town were one. But his destination was not Somorika. It was, he had been told, the first of the seven nodes of Gafaru at the foot of the first of the three hills. He had not come all that way to stop at the foot of the hill. He sought directions.

"To get to Gafaru," he was told, "you'll have to take the bush path out of Somorika and travel east until you arrive at Ika. You should not stop but must go west, past Guosa, until you arrive at Alamoza. There, you have to pass the night in the village square. Alamoza, is the half-way town between Little Gafaru and Greater Gafaru. All the seven towns are Gafarus. But you who have come without a compass, you must begin at Alamoza, the crest of the first of the three hills. There, you must sleep in the square every night until your revelation comes. Alamoza is the passageway into Gafaru, but it is also Gafaru."

He slept in the nondescript square at Alamoza for four nights. On the fourth night, he had a dream visitation by seven gray hairs. They sat around him in a circle and told him stories that began at the end and ended at the beginning. When he awoke, he sought clarification.

"The visitation means the clan of gray hairs will resolve your quest," he was told. "There are seven such clans in all the seven Gafarus. It means you must journey beyond Alamoza, past Indigo, the crest of the second hill. After Indigo, you must go further, beyond Tamara on the ascent of the third hill, until you get to the last of the Gafarus, Miitara, on the top of the third hill. There, you must seek out the shrine of the thorn god."

He discovered Miitara to be a small settlement which, like all the other Gafarus, ringed a massive shrine – one sculpted with thorns. Everyone had a gray strand or several more in his hair. Almost everyone was an acolyte of sorts, although each person – apart from the seven gray hairs who were the shrine keepers – was also a farmer or a shepherd. Within all of Gafaru, he had learned, barter was the mode of trade. But in both Somorika and Miitara, the first and the last villages, could be found trade ambassadors who ventured into the "outside world" and traded with money. It was from them that he acquired the four goats the shrine keepers demanded for his "first cleansing."

On the third day, after the cleansing, he sat in the middle of the magic circle cast by the seven gray hairs. In front of each was a bowl of incense. An acolyte sat behind each priest. His sitting position placed him in front of the shrine. At the center was a thorn sculpture. As he watched, the chief priest brought his palms gently together. The acolytes began to play a tune with local instruments. The old men now began their invocations, one after the other, and finally as one. Etiebet heard a crackle, then a tongue of flame appeared on the sculpture as if in response to the invocation.

"You have arrived, pilgrim. So says Miitara," announced the First Gray Hair. "Ours is to heal the inner person by refining it in the crucible of its higher self. She who has left you, pilgrim, she will also come back to you."

"She will?" Did he really want her back? Well, did he not? *In that sense, love is a disease, and incurable.*

"I see your beard all long and gray and she rippling with youth – the meeting of dusk and dawn."

"How can that be? I'm only a year older than she is. And I don't keep a beard."

"It shall be, pilgrim. So says Miitara."

"But I have not come for her. I'm not even sure I still want her back."

"That which you wanted and that which you want are one. When she comes back, she would have been cleansed."

He did not quite comprehend. He asked, instead, the question that had been bothering him: "Seven is the sign of victory. What went wrong in my own case?"

It was the Second Gray Hair that responded this time: "Life teems with duality. Your seven, nevertheless, was the seven of victory, of freedom from deception and false friends."

"Well said, but how does that help me? I might as well have died on that night."

"Her departure has brought you to Gafaru, to the fulfillment of your destiny. Says the dust of the road: the lore of tourists is of destinations, that of pilgrims of arrivals. The road is both brief and eternal."

"What destiny? I came here in search of comprehension."

"Life is a continual flight from the Alone to the Alone," said the Third Gray Hair. "How can you, a mere mortal, comprehend the limitless mind of the universe? We promise no such revelations. But to know one's appointed place in life is to know one's self. And to follow it and to enhance it is to achieve fulfillment. The roads of life are paved with thorns – to prick us to rise above ourselves."

"I was told that the magic of Gafaru never fails."

"And it will never fail. Many of those who come to Gafaru – that is, those who do not get duped by fraudsters – are healed. Some bathe in the Blood River – either to forget or to remember. You too could do so and then go back home and find her waiting. That is also the magic of Gafaru. But the greater magic is that which integrates you into the flow of Life Triumphant."

The tempo of the music quickened.

"'A man of the book will come up the mountains of Miitara, his heart sore and wanting that which he does not even know,'" said the Fourth Gray Hair. "'His appearance will mark the beginning of the renewal of the clan. So says the Blood River.' You are the man of the book. Your coming to Gafaru had been long foretold."

"And what was I supposed to come for?"

"To begin a new clan, which will become the ambassadors of Gafaru to the outside world."

"Me?"

"'And the new initiate,'" began the Fifth Gray Hair, "'will gather six other priests and they will interpret Gafaru to the world. For the time is coming when stone-throwers will cast their measuring gazes toward Gafaru. So says the Blood River.'"

"Am I bound to follow this prophecy?"

"No one can bind us but ourselves – our desires and our fears. But nothing can save you from your destiny, pilgrim, especially now. Gafaru is your destiny. You can leave, but now that you are here you can never depart."

"But you said Lola will come back to me. How then will that be?"

"'And the clan head of the Long Beards will so pacify the stone-throwers that their measuring gazes will transform into reverence,'" said the Sixth Gray Hair. "'But after the renewal of all the seven Gafarus, there will arrive a seductress who will ravish and sentence to perdition many priests in all the Gafarus. When this seductress comes before the clan head of the Long Beards, her tricks will avail her not. He will sacrifice her to the wind god in four directions to cleanse the mountains of renewal. And it will be his last sacrifice. So says the Blood River.'"

It began to drizzle.

"They are told – the chapters of your destiny," said the Seventh Gray Hair, the chief priest. "The next step is yours. Only you can heal yourself. Should you stay, your tutelage will properly commence after your second cleansing. For those who, because rejected, have acquired the habit of rejecting, the way forward may be to return to the past through the road of the future."

What was it Simi had told him – to get out into the open country and let the wind blow in his hair and the waves pound in his ears? Gafaru was certainly proving to be no countryside holiday. G-a-f-a-r-u: the mountains of renewal. He had left for Gafaru convinced that he had turned his back on the past. And, there, as if in rhythmic progression, a new door had opened.

In the flame, he saw the four directions open to him and the four indicative gestures. He rose up, then prostrated before the shrine.

"O Gafaru," he said.

The flame became a leap of fire, the music became celebratory, and the drizzle rainfall. In his consciousness, All became One.

—

1994

The Legend of Jonah

In the thinking of the residents of Coconut Island, it was the first place God made. Which was why, they said, He had blessed the place exceedingly. Both the river between and the earth within teemed with the bounteousness of nature. Its harvest was the most plentiful for miles around. To the many tourists who flocked to its lavish beaches and the cocoons of its wanton women, Coconut Island was also known as "The Lush Island of Pleasures." It was the "New Eden" where, instead of an Original Sin, there was an Original Pleasure – the enchantments of the ocean-finger; the coastal fraternity of diverse semi-nomads; the breezy orgasms of a tidal Communion. For, in Coconut Island, the season of the long tide was marked with beach carousels and sexual conjugations.

For its many fishermen and farmers, the demands of commerce meant a shuttle between the island and the Marina where their fishes and coconuts fetched better prices. The traffic also flowed from the Marina to the island where the sailors came to revel in the delights of The Blue Whale: The Bar for Mariners; the tourists to swim in the ocean-finger; the archaeologists to search for traces of submerged cities; and the evangelists to bring the Word to "the heathens of Eden" – the resounding description preferred by one who bore the name of Jonah.

Now the word of the Lord came to Jonas son of Amathi, saying: "Arise, and go to Ninive the great city and preach in it: for the wickedness thereof is come up before me."

Jonah was to become the most legendary among the different evangelists who came to Coconut Island. He was the only one who founded a church on the island: The Church of Jonah. It was so called, he would quote from a book, "because Jonah prophesied and prefigured in his own person the death and resurrection of Christ and was the only one among the prophets that was sent to preach to the Gentiles."

"That is also why I was named after the great prophet of the time of Jeroboam the Second," he often added.

The Jonah that came to Coconut Island was not beyond flaunting his knowledge of "the Good Book," especially the four chapters of the prophecy of Jonah and the twenty-two chapters of the Revelations. He was a personable fellow with boundless energy whose God was principally "the God of signs and wonders."

On the days the Holy Spirit came upon Jonah, which were not infrequent, he had a habit of conjuring salvation out of unlikely places. He would thrust out the mud-caked bottom of his trousers and beseech his congregation to "take thy salvation." And many there were who would rush to kiss their salvation out of the mud-caked trousers of Jonah. His legend began.

On other days, Jonah had a way of retelling stock jokes and infusing them with "the breath of the Lord." In the belief of many of the residents of Coconut Island, an Italian sailor indeed once came to The Blue Whale to pick up a woman for the night. The next morning, he gave her crisp currency notes and sent her on her way. As the girl climbed out of the ship into a canoe, the sailor could no longer hold his cry of victory. "*Senorita,* counterfeit *originale,*" he shouted as if sticking his tongue out at her. She, too, had been managing to hold herself back. "*Senor, senor,* syphilis *originale,*" she replied. Jonah would retell the story in such a way that the sailor and the woman experience a revelation and, out of the depths of their anguish, one hurls at the other: "*Senorita,* Satan *originale*"; the other responds: "*Senor, senor,* Lucifer apocalypsé."

The legend of Jonah also incorporated his choice of songs. When he was not leading his congregation to declare and to insist "Today today, my Lord will answer me today today," he led them to proclaim: "Jesus na big man. Who no know am dey call am small boy." When he was not beseeching his God not to disgrace him, he was either "claiming" a divine gift or binding the ubiquitous "evil spirits and principalities."

"O, my brethren and sisters," Jonah would exhort his congregation, "Our Lord is good; he is sweet – like rare wine. Three hearty shouts for the Lord: Hip! Hip! Hip! Hurrah!"

Jonah would then begin one of his favorite songs:

In my Father's house, there are many mansions there

In my Father's house above

"And I tell you today, brethren and sisters of Jesus, that I, Jonah, I have many many mansions, many many limousines in my father's house above. For every good thing you do in this world, you store up for yourself immense pleasures in heaven. And on the day of judgment, great shall your reward be, great shall your joy be. Brethren and sisters of Jesus, let's make a joyful noise unto the Lord."

And the legend of Jonah grew. So, too, the legend of Jonah's heaven.

For all his "confidence in the Lord of Hosts," however, Jonah had a mortal fear of the ocean-finger between the island and the Marina. He rarely ventured to the beaches. On the increasingly infrequent occasions he took a canoe ride out or into the island, he was quite a sight to behold. His garments plastered all over with crucifixes, Jonah would sing and proclaim the mercy of God in between binding "evil spirits and principalities" all through the journey. To those who wondered at this dread, he would sometimes make a confession of sorts: "Water is older than I am." He would also quickly add: "But God is more ancient than all the rivers and oceans."

Jonah's conquest of the ocean-finger was to become a part of his legend. On one of his rare trips out of Coconut Island, the rickety canoe he was traveling in hit a strong wave and was ripped apart. Those who could swim leaped out of the wooden contraption and made for the beckoning shore. Jonah, who had begun to fart uncontrollably, wept for his life with characteristic energy. As he sank into the water and was rewarded with a hungry gurgle, something in him "found the Lord who faileth not." Had Jesus, and Peter, not walked on water?

And Peter, making answer, said: Lord, if it be thou, bid me come to thee upon the waters. And he said: Come. And Peter going down out of the boat walked upon the water to come to Jesus.

Imploring the Lord not to disgrace him, Jonah bound all the turbulent evil spirits and principalities, postponed his journey to claim his mansions and limousines in heaven, and leaped out of the deep like a whale. The consequent legend has many variations, the favorite one being that Jonah floated out of the water with his mouth "glorifying the Lord" and his former drowning companions saved by clinging to his garment. The legend of Jonah grew into the legend of Coconut Island.

In the victory service he held, on the beach, the preacher spoke interminably about faith – that which could move mountains.

"And I tell you, brethren and sisters of Jesus, that you too can do it. I, Jonah, I conquered the ocean-finger, which is older than me, by the grace of God which I claimed through faith. You, too, you can!" So impassioned was the pastor that he gesticulated wildly as he spoke. "If you have been lying around wallowing in sickness, in poverty, in suffering, I tell you today: you are a f-o-o-l. The earth is our Lord's, and the fullness thereof. It is for the son or the daughter to claim the riches of the father."

Jonah's excessive passion during that first sermon at the beach must have struck Ashikodi, the head-walker of Coconut Island, as rather humorous. Ashikodi was known to haunt the beach as much as Jonah stayed away from the area. Unlike the legend of Jonah, Ashikodi's legend was anchored on his professed belief – "one world at a time."

"Rather a visible bungalow on earth than an invisible mansion in heaven," he was known to sneer.

"You're a candidate for hell," Jonah often told him.

"Rather that than a fool's paradise," he would fire back.

The times Ashikodi sang about heaven at all, it was to echo the Negro spiritual:

> When I get to Heaven gonna put on my shoes
> I'm gonna walk all over God's heaven

He had heard about Jonah's conquest of the ocean-finger, but he found the preacher's chest-thumping comical. Unable to hold back any longer, he broke into laughter and began to walk on his head. An infuriated Jonah summoned all his immense energy, claimed a chunk from his huge reservoir of divine gifts, and tried to cast out Ashikodi.

But the head-walker would not go away. Instead, he righted himself and challenged the pastor to a swimming contest.

"And will you accept the Lord Jesus as your Lord and savior thereafter, you troubler of Coconut Island?"

"If you win."

And Elias said again to the people: I only remain, a prophet of the Lord: but the prophets of Baal are four hundred and fifty men. Let two bullocks be given us, and let them choose one bullock for themselves, and cut it in pieces and lay it upon wood, but put no fire under and I will dress the other bullock, and lay it on wood, and put no fire under it. Call ye on the names of your gods, and I will call on the name of my Lord: and the God that shall answer by fire, let him be God. And all the people answering said: A very good proposal.

Jonah kneeled down and invoked "the Lord who faileth not." In his passion, he exchanged several of his mansions and limousines for extra divine gifts. When he was through with the transaction, he beckoned to Ashikodi, who had been busy showing off his head-walking skills, and leaped into the water. At first, Jonah managed to tag behind his rival but, soon, with Ashikodi far out in the water, it became apparent that Jonah was engaged in a sermon unto death. Tossed up and down the ancient ocean-finger, each attempt of his to cry out even more forcefully meant an even larger gulp of water. By the time a rescue team managed to drag him out of the ocean-finger, they discerned that the pastor had gone to claim his remaining limousines and mansions in his "Father's house above."

It is a sumptuous palace, just as Jonah had always envisioned. The gleaming gates rise into the sky; they pronounce a personalized welcome: "Welcome to heaven, Jonah, victorious laborer in the vineyard of Coconut Island." The welcome brings a smile to the addressee's face. The gates swing open to admit him, and he is immediately possessed by the celestial music of the welcoming choir of angels: "Glory be, glory be to the Lord of Hosts and they that walk in his path." Jonah breaks into a whirling dance. In his animated elation, he walks on his head. "Fellow brethren and sisters of Jesus," he hosannas. "Today is the day that the Lord has made."

The roads are paved with gold. There are mansions and mansions everywhere the keen eyes of Jonah look. The gardens have been manicured with stunning precision. The air is so rarefied that it is as if it has been raked clean. Everything visible gleams unbelievably. Every sound has a deep resonance.

The choir of angels lead Jonah up to an imposing Bank of Heaven. Again, there is a personalized welcome: "Pay Pastor Jonah, lately of Coconut Island, the sum of eight mansions and sixteen limousines." Inspired, Jonah makes joyful noises unto the Lord. As they turn away from the bank, new inscriptions light up hitherto unnamed mansions: Jonah...Jonah...Jonah...In the driveway of each mansion are two elegant limousines.

Later – morning? noon? night? – it strikes Jonah that it is for him to prepare his meals, drive and wash the limousines, and generally take care of himself. Really? There are no personal servants in heaven? He had secured several mansions and limousines without managing to secure housekeepers and chauffeurs. But the thought initiates its fulfillment. Platters of various dishes appear on his dining table. A grateful Jonah falls to. Thereafter, belch after heavenly belch, he sets out on an exploratory tour.

The air is charged with "Hallelujahs" and "hosannas." Jonah, too, no longer walks. He dances his way about in the lilting manner of the welcoming angels. He had donned on one of the gleaming unisex robes he had discovered that the wardrobes of his mansions were filled with. In the middle of a large square, an angel – the town crier? – is announcing, in-between gong beats: "And the Patriarch of Heaven has proclaimed the Season of Laughter." Correspondingly, the angel ends the announcement with a guffaw. Jonah is almost flooded by rivers of laughter which converge on him from all sides and infect him. He begins a serial laughter that progresses from transparency into opacity. All around him, he sees huge signs laughing in the aerial voids of heaven: "Proclaimed by the Patriarch: A Heaven of Laughters."

His feet lead him to the monumental amphitheater he had seen listed in the catalog on his sitting room table as "the Window of Heaven, capacity: 1,444,000." From his seat in the cavernous dome, from which the citizens of heaven watch the happenings on earth, the vista of earth is spread out like pinpoints of light. He focuses his thought, and Coconut Island appears before his gaze. He sees himself – the other Jonah – being readied for burial. He hears all the prayers for the repose of his soul. But he also reads in the hearts of many in the congregation wishes for his restoration to life. Foolish souls, he wishes he could still teach them a thing or two about prayers. *Catalog of Heaven, entry No.18: "Precision is the lesser key of prayers. Be it known to you, o citizens of heaven, that the shuttle between heaven and earth only admits one theme per minute per week. All other questing themes are dissipated into rain or storm clouds." Appendage: 10,080 themes. Catalog of Heaven, entry No. 19: "And faith is the greater key of prayers. Be it known to you, o citizens of heaven, that the channel between the earth and the Throne Room of the Patriarch admits only prayers anchored on the rock of faith. All others are dissipated into purgatory."*

Jonah's eyes search out Ashikodi on the fringe of the congregation. He has apparently mastered new head-walking tricks. He is walking on his head down the beach with his legs making acrobatic movements in the air. The "troubler of Coconut Island" has also mastered new songs – "songs of erotic frankness," he calls them – modeled on the rhythm of Christian hymns. Jonah forgets all the injunctions of the Catalog. How many times had he asked God to take Ashikodi "in hand"? How many times? Yet it was he, "the interpreter of the ways of God to man," that had drowned – drowned? – while Ashikodi had triumphed. He wishes he can send a thunderbolt to solve "the Ashikodi problem" once for all. *Catalog of Heaven, entry No. 3: "Only in the form of assistance, certainly not punishment, can the citizens of heaven relate with the inhabitants of earth."*

A thousand streaks of lightning rolled into one courses through the amphitheater, causing a most dazzling sensation and a great stillness. In this quietude comes the announcement – as if at the departure hall of an airport: "Attention, ladies and gentlemen. This is to announce that Jonah, lately of Coconut Island, is wanted immediately at the Throne Room of the Patriarch. This is a call for Jonah, lately of Coconut Island, to report immediately to the Throne of the Patriarch. Thank you." Jonah is nonplussed. *Catalog of Heaven, entry No. 2: "New arrivals can only see God after one full season – for a formal initiation into the entire epical dimensions of heaven."* Why then is he being summoned? Why is he being so summoned? Has he so soon merited promotion?

His first view of the Throne Room triggers an assault on his psyche. It is an alabaster monument sculpted like nubile nipples. Nipples? On the walls are seemingly sensual murals that cause an involuntary arousal in the being of Jonah. In consequence, when he is admitted before the presence of the Patriarch, he stands with his face downward like one of the fallen angels he had seen in the Catalog.

"Jonah," rumbles the thunder of the Patriarch, "lift up your eyes, Jonah, and behold the face of heaven."

It is the face of a patriarch ringed in the lower region by a luminous, golden beard. Around the portly being on an incandescent throne are beatific angels massaging his different aspects. Jonah wonders greatly at this sight. There is something about the scene that faintly conjures the interior of the Blue Whale he had occasionally espied in passing.

"For so long, Jonah, have I tended you so that you will know My ways," the Golden Beard addresses him once more. "But, on earth, you were like a fig – stripped of flesh by the world to come. And this is that world. But, in holy art, you Jonah see worldly embraces. In our hallowed spheres, you, Jonah, think of avenging thunderbolts and airport voices. When then will you learn, Jonah, that all things must pass away except My Word, which was in the beginning?"

Jonah has overcome a measure of his shame and his dread. "But, Lord," he protests, "did I not ceaselessly preach Your Word?"

"How much did you, Jonah, truly understand and believe?"

"I believed, O Lord, although...although I had my problems with certain aspects. Many many times there were when I wondered: If Adam and Eve were the first people You created and Cain and Abel were their initial offspring, who then did Cain marry to bring forth Henoch? How could Noah's ark – three hundred cubits in length, fifty cubits in breadth and thirty cubits in height – have contained him and his family and a pair of every living creature? Many many times there were that I wondered about certain aspects of Your Word."

"But never did you preach your inner truth or share your wonderment, Jonah. Where was your faith in the larger mysteries of the Word?"

"O Lord, yet I believed."

"Thou shalt not lie."

"But, O Lord..."

"And how many times did you reduce Me into a deaf God, Jonah, who must be noised to? How many times did you fractionalize Me into the God of Jonah and the God of Ashikodi, the God of Coconut Island and the God of the Marina? And when did you ever not relate to Me as an exploiter of the 'God of Signs and Wonders,' a creditor of 'the Lord Who Faileth Not'?"

"But, O Lord, it is for the son to claim the riches of his father."

"Who empowered you, Jonah, to judge and segregate My children?"

"But, O Lord, many there are, like Ashikodi, who do not walk in Your ways. Mine was the Great Commission – to shine the light for 'the heathens of Eden' and prepare them for the Rapture. I cast my net far and wide, O Lord, and so very diligently did I fish for lost souls."

"'Thou shalt love the Lord thy God with thy whole heart and with thy whole soul and with thy whole mind. This is the greatest and the first commandment. And the second is like to this: Thou shalt love thy neighbor as thyself. On these two commandments dependeth the whole law and the prophets.'"

"I know, O Lord."

"How many times did you quote unto your congregation: 'I am the Lord thy God...Thou shalt not have strange gods before me' – even when you made yourself a god over them?"

"But, O Lord, I was only shepherding them against wolves."

"And you shepherded them with oaths and decrees and damnation? How many times, Jonah, did you lay with nudists during the Communion of the Long Tide?"

"Never, O Lord. Never."

"In your thoughts and cravings, you lay severally with every one of them, you hypocrite. You are what you are, Jonah. You are what you crave. Neither be ashamed nor hypocritical about life and its currents. You are, therefore, to return to earth and learn anew the lessons of life."

A displeased Jonah opens his mouth to speak, but he is already traveling down a great void. Nevertheless, he sprays his response into the fabulous darkness: "And I tell you, O Lord of Beatific Angels, there must have been a mistake. I must have been sent to the wrong heaven and summoned before a Non-Testament God. I am Jonah, arch apostle of the God of the New Testament. I have no business with the earth anymore, with the Ashikodis of the world. What business has light with darkness?"

And they took Jonas and cast him into the sea: and the sea ceased from raging...Now the Lord prepared a great fish to swallow up Jonas: and Jonas was in the belly of the fish three days and three nights. And Jonas prayed to the Lord his God out of the belly of the fish...I am cast away out of thy eyes: but yet I shall see thy holy temple again...And the Lord spoke to the fish: and it vomited out Jonas upon the dry land.

Jonah came to just in time to hear the lid of the coffin slammed shut. He could hear even the voice of Ashikodi singing among other voices:

> Resurrection, resurrection
> By the power of God
>   the spirit of God
> The love of God is manifest
> The love of God is manifest
>   in me

Jonah was no longer in the foul mood he had been in upon his deportation. He had been imbued with a new wisdom founded on his reflections during his return journey. But he was in a great hurry to get out of the coffin, which he could sense was already being ominously lifted up. He heaved outward with a great tide of strength. The lid flew up the same moment the pallbearers must have let go. The contraption thudded on the ground with such brutal force that Jonah sat up clutching his waist and wondering if all his bones still retained the status quo.

Everyone was in flight. Jonah stood astride his coffin flailing his hands in all directions as he beseeched the vanishing assembly: "I entreat you to return, O brothers and sisters in Christ. It's me, Jonah, returned from a great error of a journey. And I tell you this day: vanity upon vanity, all is vanity."

Ashikodi tarried awhile, long enough to shout: "Heaven is personal." Then he too sped away. But he was also the first to return to listen to the returnee's passionate sermon.

And the legend of Jonah traveled, like the fabled smoke cloud, right up to heaven's gate.

—

1994

The Honorable Fartheads

Ime Uduak, Honorable Member of Parliament, managed to stifle a yawn until the parliament recessed, then he yawned his way out of the chamber. His restraint, as he saw it, had been the politically correct option under the circumstances. Should he have yawned while his party's Chief Whip had been belaboring the notion of his constituency as "educationally disadvantaged"?

Uduak, the representative of the Kali District in the Federal House of Representatives, believed in his party. It was more than just the AP – the Advancement Party – to him. It was *the* Party, the only one out of the four parties approved by the national electoral body that deserved italicization and capitalization. It was the Party that had catapulted him into parliament. It was the Party that had finagled his victory in a controversial second-term election. It was the Party in power. And Bante Lam, its Chief Whip in the House, was one of its formidable leaders.

Bante Lam had rooted for Uduak in the party primaries when his ambition had been dangerously challenged by better-known opponents. He had taught him how to win an election regardless of the actual votes. So, after his first four-year term, during which time he never made the several rescheduled trips to his constituency, he had won a second term without as much as uttering a campaign promise. Bante Lam had handled the consequent dispute and litigation. Should he, therefore, have yawned while his political godfather had been enunciating for the hundredth instant the notion of his constituency as "educationally disadvantaged" and therefore "qualified" for "enhanced educational incentives"?

"With your permission, Mr. Speaker, I want to remind this honorable House that my people – the Kasuwas of the Niger Valley – have no schools. And, much worse, they have never had. More than thirty years of political independence have meant no schools, no scholarships, no significant development for my people, the Kasuwas of the Niger Valley. Where then lies the honor of this acclaimed

House of the People if it considers the bill on development incentives without remarking that my constituency – the Kasuwas of the Niger Valley – have been educationally disadvantaged since Adam and Eve and are therefore eminently qualified for enhanced educational incentives? With your permission, Mr Speaker, I urge this honorable House to speak to the future with a due knowledge of the past."

Outside the parliament building, after yawning, Ime Uduak congratulated Bante Lam for "another landmark motion."

"I'm sure that it'll receive the blessing of the House," he added.

"Oh, I try," the burly Chief Whip said. "If only my constituents, the Kasuwas of the Niger Valley, know the lengths I go to on their behalf..."

"They will return you to parliament with a landslide victory forever and ever."

"I assure you that I have no aspiration to forever be a parliamentarian, my boy. One must think of bigger things."

"Pardon my naiveté."

Even as he played, as he saw it, the politically correct role of congratulating Bante Lam once more, Uduak could see on the screen of his mind the true state of the "House of the People." Every member had his own favorite motion which he proposed at every possible opportunity. And because virtually every motion was answered, as stoutly, with a contrary one, very few bills – mostly of little consequence – had received the approval of the House in the six years that he had been there. For every Bante Lam, there was a J. I. D. Asalam, the Minority Leader.

"Mr Speaker Sir...Fellow Honorables, I have the floor, please! As I was saying before I was interrupted, Mr Speaker, it is not only the Kasuwas of the Niger Valley who are educationally marginalized. May I remind this House that the first school in Nigeria was established in Rifuwa District one hundred years ago. Since independence, no other school or scholarship or significant development has been channeled to this district. If we are here in the name of an independent nation, then it is pertinent to note that the people of Rifuwa District have also gained nothing from that political independence. The Honorable

Bante Lam speaks of disadvantage, but how can there be disadvantage where there has been no advantage? In the case of the Kasuwas of the Niger Valley, the status quo has remained. For the Rifuwas, the experience has been much worse. If any place is eminently qualified for enhanced educational incentives, it is Rifuwa District and other such first-generation academic zones. This parliament is not about rewriting the chapters of Genesis...Fellow Honorables, I still have the floor, please!"

"And I hope I will always be right, at least in politics, despite the machinations of the Jidases of this world," Lam said to Uduak reflectively. *Jidas* was Bante Lam's chosen corruption of the Minority Leader's initials. "If his people had had schools since the beginning of the world, what more does he want? The end of the world as a school play in Rifuwa District?"

"I think he's a climber, chief. And he wants to use you as a ladder."

"Are you telling me? I know his type. The turning of the parliament is approaching once more. I'll cut him down to size this time."

The "turning of the parliament," as Uduak knew, was the phrase for the term-end coups and counter coups engineered by the parliamentarians to clip the wings of their arch opponents at the polls and thus bar their return to the parliament. Even those like Bante Lam, Ime Uduak, and J. I. D. Asalam who were serving their second terms could also be hurt this way, especially with respect to their future political ambitions. Lam, who often boasted that he had mastered the art of *magicking* electoral victories, was professedly unafraid of the turning of the parliament.

"But I pity the anti-Lams," he would proclaim with disdain.

The "anti-Lams," in his lexicon, were all those whose countermotions had set up barrier after barrier against the passage of the Chief Whip's favorite whip of a motion. In the long list of such fellow honorables, none riled the burly magician as much as Inua Saheli. Saheli, who was serving his first term in parliament, was the most vocal member of the Future Party, the least popular of the four parties. The Future Party preached "Futurism" as the way forward "after decades of visionlessness."

"Once more, Mr Speaker Sir, the House is caught between Bante Lam and J. I. D. Asalam, two formidable honorables. But the issue should not be whether the Kasuwas of the Niger Valley have had no schools ever or whether Rifuwa District has had its schools decimated by government neglect or official thoughtlessness. This parliament is bigger than both constituencies, and such narrow contentions should be dealt with at the level of the Houses of Assembly in the states. The issue is that our educational system is in shambles and, in some places such as the Sahel District, which I represent, yet to be properly instituted. In the Niger Valley, in Rifuwa District, in Sahel District, in virtually every district in this country, the education sector is gasping. This is the larger concern that this House should address and not dwell unnecessarily on the 'I the people' posturing of Bante Lam, especially, and J. I. D. Asalam, both nevertheless formidable honorables."

"And that Saheli, I'll break him before I'm through. If I can understand, sometimes, a political stalwart like J. I. D. Jidas acting out the anti-Lam opposition, the presumptuousness of that little Sahel rat sticks in my throat. What does he know about politics? What does he know about anything? He talks of the larger interest, as if his understanding or interest is greater than that of the House. The parliament is the entire country in three hundred constituencies. If I speak I speak as Kasuwa District. I speak as an important part of a whole. Where is the posturing in that? Imagine the cheek of describing me, 'especially,' as a posturer. He's done for."

Uduak managed to make some politically correct noise, promised to attend a meeting of the Lam faction of the Party that night and left. He always found Saheli as a subject rather troubling.

When he came to the parliament six years ago, he had been somewhat like Inua Saheli – a defiant advocate of the common good, of the free and fair, and all other such notions that constituted what Saheli routinely described as "essential futurism, though party affiliations may differ." But he had reckoned without Bante Lam. The Chief Whip had watched Uduak for some time before he counseled him to "mend" his ways.

"I'm sure that in your mind you're some sort of Samson. It's a common beginner's disease – the delusion of grandeur," he told him. "But you're making a big mistake. Things won't change just because you want them to or because you've moved three hundred and sixty-five progressive motions in a year. Things will only begin to change when the military stop tampering with democracy, when voters begin to pay attention to political programs instead of ancestral history, when the judiciary and the executive arms change, when...when this world as we know it comes to an end. Meanwhile, you can be more useful to yourself and to your party and even to your constituency than you have been so far by learning political correctness."

"Things will begin to change when lawmakers begin to make just and progressive laws," he countered. "I'm not the world, only a part of it. But if I can polish my part, and everyone else does the same, it'll be a radiant world."

"I am Bante Lam. It is not for nothing that I supported your bid, despite your hallucinations. You are young and intelligent. You are Bante Lam several years ago. You will learn and then you will bend down and see Nigeria."

But he did not bend, not immediately. Over the next few months, he kept up his advocacies and strictly relied only on the allowances that parliamentarians were paid and the money he made from his law chambers. Then, one evening, Bante Lam came to see him in his quarters. He had a commission from the Presidency to push a bill through, and he was trying to win over the likes of Uduak.

"I'm not going to beat about the bush with you, Uduak," he told him. "I need your support – or your silence or even your absence – to get this bill through. You will be well-paid. If you will not do it for money, then do it as a favor for my help during the primaries."

"I can't, chief. I remain grateful to you, but I won't sell my conscience."

To his surprise, Bante Lam burst into laughter. "You foolish boy," he said, "I knew you would say something like not selling your conscience – as if I'm some sort of devil and your conscience is a valuable commodity. Well, take care of your conscience. Remember: I came to you first."

It was not until the next day when the police burst into his quarters that he understood the import of Bante Lam's words. He was in bed with a young woman who had surprised him that evening by seducing him. Inside his quarters, she had led him on until they were both naked, in bed, before she erupted into blood-curdling screams. The police burst in as if on cue and, within minutes, had Uduak "under arrest for rape." "I will not bend," Uduak swore to himself and to everyone else. How he wished he had denounced Bante Lam publicly! And why had he, rather than contend with imminent defeat, ever accepted Lam's political goodwill in the first place?

In the court, it was obvious that the case was going against him. But what finally broke his resolve was his demonization by the media, which had enthusiastically hailed him once upon a time. The initial question marks quickly became exclamation points. Every aspect of his private life was exhumed and tailored to fit the new image of him as a maniac. He was set to lose in all possible courts – of public opinion, of Justice Kilenko, of the parliament. *What is the worth of righteous advocacies in a country of bloodthirsty savages? What is the point of insisting on the narrow path when the people applaud only the highway to ruin?* Questions, questions. He saw amplified in the fickleness of the sensation-crazy media the flakiness of the people, their rather shortsighted adulation of power and money-gods.

It was Bante Lam who came with an answer – "a new deal," as he put it. "Look at you now, Samson. I bow and tremble before you," he said lightheartedly. "Look, Uduak, I have nothing against you personally. When you came to me for help, I gave it unstintingly. So, this is not about you and me. It's the system in motion. Certainly, you are headed for ruin, but I'll tell you something, my friend. We can make a new deal. You see how your friends and fellow advocates in the media have scavenged your past, and your future even, for choice commercial morsels? But your record has worked for you in this one important respect: it has upped your price. You are a cunning devil, sure. Mend your ways and we'll have the case against you withdrawn, finance a cleanup campaign in the media, and generally take care of you. You name your price. Remember what I told you before? Bend down and you will see Nigeria."

Uduak made the deal. The case was dropped. Retractions and apologies appeared in the press. And showers of government contracts fell on him. He had bent down and, indeed, he saw Nigeria – the Nigeria of lavish dinner meetings in five-star hotels; the Nigeria of billion-naira reconstruction contracts; of vote-drunk megalomaniacs. He saw, and he became. But, once upon a time, he had been like Inua Saheli – full of certainties and scornful of rationalizations.

When Ime Uduak, Honorable Member of Parliament, arrived at his law chambers, there was a solitary letter waiting for him. Both the number and the impoverished, travel-weary appearance of the envelope were unusual. He slit it open, drew out a single sheet of paper, and began to read with increasing astonishment:

"Our son, the Honorable Ime Uduak,

"Greetings. We write to express our unflinching solidarity with you in this period of trial. We have heard that you supposedly raped a young woman and that you are facing trial in the capital city. The Great Juju of Kali says that you are innocent. We are, therefore, planning to march on the capital to press for your release and honorable reinstatement as our representative.

"We enjoin you not to waver. Remember at all times where you come from and what you represent. We are peasant farmers and hunters, perhaps the poorest people in the entire country, and we want development. You, our son, the product of a community scholarship, should never waver in your struggle to bring the torch of progress home to Kali so that we too and those who will come after us will see the light. Always remember your great commission."

The letter was signed by the Elders Council. There was a postscript assuring him that his sole living parent, his father, was in good health.

Was this a cruel joke? Quickly, he scrutinized the date on the letter. It was written the same week his trial had commenced six years ago. He studied the postmark. The letter had apparently been posted the same week. And it had arrived six years late! To think of what this expression of solidarity might have accomplished! He called in his secretary – a young, efficient woman – and interrogated her closely. She knew no more than that the letter had been delivered that morning.

The letter took Uduak's mind back to the last time he visited Kali six years ago. He had gone, after the election, on a thank-you tour and had promised the people "a thousand points of light." The headmaster of the sole, decaying school in the district and its public letter writer had joked that only a point or two during his term in parliament would suffice. Kali was a typical backwoods district – no electricity, no pipe-borne water, a solitary dispensary, and a crumbling elementary school in Kali, the principal village. It was in that elementary school that Uduak had distinguished himself and earned a community scholarship that paid for his high school and university education. His visits to Kali since then had been infrequent and, since that thank-you tour, not at all. When he decided to contest the election, he had the plight of the district uppermost at heart. And he had initiated a number of motions with that consideration in mind in his first six months as a parliamentarian.

"Thank you, Mr Speaker, for your recognition. I want to propose a Village Reclamation Bill. Our villages are dying. In Kali District, which I represent, the decay acquires an even more frightening dimension with each new day. Mr Speaker, I protest that my people are dying. They have been dying for a long time. But they are part of Nigeria, and so are several others like them nationwide. We have to reclaim these villages and integrate them into the mainstream of development. I propose, therefore, a New Life Scheme for our rural areas that will bring development closer to the people."

The proposal had been talked away. And now, several years afterward, this letter! His people had cared when he had believed that no one did. But what was it worth – a shaft of light permeating through a six-year darkness? In the end, he firmed his decision to go home –

one that he had somewhat arrived at in the preceding months. He had also become a calculating political machine and had come to realize that Bante Lam's influence could only take him as far as he had come. In two years, he planned to run for governorship in his home state. It was time to begin building or expanding his political base – starting from his home district. The decision finally firmly made, he consulted his schedules, factored in the fact of his wife's seven-month pregnancy, and dictated a telegram to the Kali Elders Council:

"Solidarity letter received six years late Stop Apologies for unavoidable absence Stop Will be home on the 26th instant to enter into a New Covenant Stop Will tour the entire state after Kali Stop Regards to papa Stop."

Two weeks afterward, on the 26th day of the month, Ime Uduak, Honorable Member of Parliament, took leave of his wife of three years in the seventh month of a long-sought pregnancy, for a "New Covenant Visit" to Kali. His briefcase bulged with currency notes. As he drove the hundreds of miles to Kali, his thoughts dwelled on the parliament.

Because of the electoral law, each parliamentarian had at least completed high school. Sometimes, the more sycophantic of the parliament's media ambassadors called it "The Educated Parliament." The House records, he knew, were filled with populist proposals and arguments but these, he also knew, were staged for the benefit of the press gallery and public opinion. The parliamentarians had a name for such eloquent dramatics: "For the Records." Such motions hardly ever passed, sure as they were to be thwarted by a maze of contrary arguments. Not so, however, motions concerning the welfare of the lawmakers.

"Mr Speaker, sir, permit me to move that the sitting allowance of the honorable members of this house be immediately doubled and, henceforth, adjusted each quarter in tune with inflationary trends nationwide."

"With your permission, Honorable Speaker, let me bring to the

attention of this honorable House my gruesome ordeal last night in my quarters. My peace was encroached upon and my health threatened by a spider which insisted on doing acrobatics on my toilet wall all night. Is it not a national shame that an entire constituency should be subjected to such an ordeal? I, therefore, move that, as a matter of the utmost urgency, a generous pest allowance be granted all honorable members for the purpose of combating such invasions."

"Mr. Speaker, sir, fellow honorables, the time has come for us to positively address the issue of the proper reference to the honorable members of this House. In this hall are gathered the representatives of all the three hundred constituencies in the country. In this hall, therefore, is gathered the entire country. It is a distinguished and honorable convocation. I move that every member of this gathering be addressed, permanently, as Honorable. I also move that all members be entitled to all their present allowances after their service in this acclaimed House of the People."

There were many such motions, and they were all passed into law. At such times, the usual divisions along party or faction lines usually disappeared. Of course, the Inua Sahelis always had something to say against such proposals, but the House was usually rather united in shouting "the Marxist pretenders" down or the Speaker firm in denying them the floor.

More often than not, however, the House was a battlefront – with the Bante Lams and the J. I. D. Asalams as the commanders of private armies. Just last night, Uduak had attended a secret meeting of the Lam faction where a plan had been perfected to "expose" Inua Saheli as a bribe-taker. The objective was to get him convicted, then impeached from the House. Poor Saheli.

On and on whirled the parliamentary mind of Ime Uduak, Honorable Member of the "House of the People" – until he turned off the highway for the last few miles of the journey. It was then that Kali finally caught up with him.

The ancient signpost was still there but tottering like a ludicrous accident and only barely managing to proclaim, through severely bleached letters: *Welcome to Kali.* Once upon a time, that signpost had been the masterpiece of a joint enterprise between the village headmaster and the blacksmith. What had once been a manageable access road knifing through Ali, the first of the hamlets in the district, was now an almost impassable track. It did not take long before Uduak's car got stuck. Try as much as he could, the car would go no further. Reluctantly, he climbed out. Clutching his briefcase, he approached four men sitting under a tree a little distance from the road. His intention was simple – to solicit their assistance. But no sooner did he approach than the men, apparently realizing who he was, bolt away with a great holler as if he were the incarnation of seven devils rolled into one.

He recovered from his amazement and, now infuriated by "the primitive reaction of these Ali savages," returned to his vehicle. With much effort, he managed to extricate the car and continue on his way. From his rearview mirror, he could see the four men returning, with what seemed like an entire village in tow. "What good can ever come out of Ali?" he muttered to himself. "Ali, you will yet recognize me properly and then you will bow."

With Ali behind, he drove up to the point where he had to turn off the road for the final stretch to Kali. But there was no road. *Where had these primitives been all these years while the rest of the world had been taking great leaps forward – mired in the ways of the oracles and the forests? What did they think peculiarly gave them the right to presume that the rest of the world owed them a service? Kali, O Kali, is this what you have done to yourself?*

He kept up the spiral of questions because of his anger and as a way of numbing his conscience. Had he not initiated great motions on their behalf? Was this age of possibilities not also the age of self-help?

Having come this far, he was determined to accomplish his mission as quickly as possible and return to civilization. In making the journey, he had also discovered, or been discovered by, the cardinal agenda of his new covenant: "Give me your votes, Kali, and I will make you breathe again. O Kali, our needs have made us politically one." So, when his car stood at the edge of the forest that had obliterated what had once been the road to his hometown, Ime Uduak, Honorable Member of Parliament, got out of the car and, clutching his briefcase, continued his journey on foot. Just a half-mile of forest, just a half-mile more. He would make a New Covenant speech out of it: "O Kali, when even the forest stood in my path, I looked it in the face and I said: 'Neither your mystique nor your thorns will separate me and my people, for Kali and I are one.'"

He had not walked any great distance before he came to a clearing. He knew instantly that he was before the Great Juju of Kali – an awe-inspiring shrine almost enshrouded by trees in which four tongues of flame communed with the dense silence. What had happened to have made the villagers move their primary oracle? "The Great Juju of Kali never moves...The Great Juju of Kali never moves...The Great Juju of Kali never moves." Such had been the unquestioning monotony with which that fact had been drilled into him as an initiate. Now, this. *O Kali, what have you done to yourself? What are you doing to yourself, Kali?* Even as the intimidating sight and its aura affected Uduak's heartbeat, his eyes fell on what was unmistakably a sacrifice – a white goat hacked into four odd parts. Ime Uduak, Honorable Member of Parliament, lost the rest of his already diminished resolve. Still managing to grip his briefcase, he blundered toward the road, crying out for salvation. But it was as if the forest had acquired its own dynamics of expansion. In as much as Uduak ran, he could not get to the road. *Kali, you Kali, what are you doing to me?*

Uduak kept up his race until he tripped and finally lay exhausted on the forest floor. When he managed to drag himself up, he discovered that his wristwatch must have been claimed by the forest in the course of his race. Because the treetops made up the ceiling of the forest, he could no longer tell what time of day it was. Uduak realized he had only one option if he was to stay alive – to firmly reject despair. The world could not have become all forest and uninhabited, he reasoned. He took great gulps of air and set off once more the way he had come. The New Covenant? Bah! *O Kali, mired even more deeply in the ways of the oracles and the forests, how can the future speak to you? With what voice can the rainbow speak to the graveyard?*

Although he did not know it, Ime Uduak, Honorable Member of Parliament, spent five days and nights in the forest walking determinedly in his waking hours toward the road – or so he thought. The first time he succumbed to sleep, he had a dream in which he found himself in a graveyard standing about ten paces away from a crack in the earth. From where he stood, he could hear a babble of voices which he recognized as those of his fellow parliamentarians engaged in a great jumble of an argument. The second time, he found himself only eight paces away from the widening opening in the earth, and the babble of contentions came to him with an even greater insistence. On and on went the progression of this new phenomenon until, at the fifth instance, he stood on the brink of what was unmistakably a grave, from which issued a fiendish rage of voices. One more step, he knew, and he would be over the brink, yet he appeared to lack the ability to control his motion.

When he awoke from the nightmare, bathed in his own sweat, he kneeled down where he had lain and invoked the pantheon of gods he had disregarded for a long time to intervene on his behalf. *O Kali, have I not come all this way to make a New Covenant with you? If I ever forget you again, Kali, if I ever ever forget you again, let my testicles recede into my groin, let thunder strike me neckless.*

After another terrible day – day? – in the forest, Uduak had another dream – dream? – in which the forest finally parted and he emerged into Kali, his hometown.

The ordeal had taken its toll. The Ime Uduak whom the forest regurgitated was a ruin of a man – shrunken, torn in several places, his parliamentary robes almost reduced to a loincloth. As he stood on the village path still clutching his briefcase and battling to get used to the sunlight, he knew that he stank and generally presented a tragicomic spectacle. He knew that he looked anything but an incarnation of the New Covenant. He noticed the gray hairs of the

Elders Council walking toward him – five gaunt, old men advancing with the help of their walking sticks as if they were apparitions. Certainly, this was no welcoming party. But...but how had they known about his coming? His telegram? Bah! Kali had obviously relapsed into that era in which telegrams could as well be futuristic intercontinental missiles.

When the Elders Council got to where he stood shamefacedly but nevertheless expecting some sort of recognition, they veered off and began to move away. There was something in their motion that willed him to follow them. And he did, still clutching his briefcase.

The silent journey terminated in the now familiar village graveyard. First, they pointed out to him his father's grave – a mound of grassy earth and a cross on which the village headmaster had written: Pa Uduak, Hunter.

"He was one of the many who died in the epidemic last year," said one of the five gaunt, old men.

"What epidemic?" Uduak wondered.

Next, they pointed out another grave, marked by a cross bearing the inscription: Ime Uduak, Politician.

"You are dead. And Kali has buried you," they told him.

Ime Uduak, Honorable Member of Parliament, knew then that he faced the toughest battle of his life. Despite his long absence from the village, he had not entirely forgotten its ways and means.

"But how can I be dead when I still live, fathers?" he said, sinking to his knees. "How could you have buried me, your son who has been fighting mighty battles for you in the capital?" *Kali, what political devil pushed me into ever making this sojourn into your clutches? What political enemy has scored this fatal landslide at my expense?*

"You were once the village, Ime, the embodiment of its hopes and aspirations. Until last year. The epidemic struck and half the people perished in utmost misery. Do you not understand that gods die when their worshippers perish? Divinity is a covenant."

The last word took hold of him. He opened his briefcase and displayed, hopefully, the mound of mint-fresh currency notes within.

"Here, fathers, you can have it all. That is why I really came – to transform your lives. Here, you can have it all."

The five gaunt, old men only looked at him scornfully.

"What have you done to yourself, Ime? Do you not understand that the village, which once stood at the edge of the forest, could have gone in one of two ways – either back into the forest or out into the road? Do you not understand that the village has receded into the forest? We have no use for your currency notes. We have gone back to bartering, back to the days of yore."

"If only you know the valiant battles I have waged in the parliament on your...on our behalf," Uduak pleaded. "I have thundered again and again: 'My people are dying.' And when I finally stood before the Great Juju...Ah, yes, how could the village have moved the Great Juju that never moves?"

"Taa! The Great Juju of Kali never moves. The Great Juju of Kali never moved. It is the world, the world of your honorable fartheads that has moved away from Kali."

What argument was possible? "I have returned, fathers. Your son has come back to you. Wash me clean with your mercy. But do not sentence me to be feasted upon by the termites and the vile beings of the underworld. Do not let Ali rejoice at the fall of Kali. Do not let Lia rejoice. Do not let Ila rejoice. Together, we will push back the forest, far far back, and we will breathe again. I have come to make a new covenant with Kali."

"Do you not understand that Kali is beyond the laughter, beyond the mockery of those who themselves also have no faces? What have you done to yourself, Ime?"

Even as he continued to plead with them, the five gaunt, old men began to walk away. Ime Uduak, Honorable Member of Parliament, fell on his face then and sobbed with all the gravity of his present condition. The swing of the capital city and the power-plays in the parliament had deceived him into a disdainful perception of Kali and its ways. But now, in the village graveyard, after his ordeal in the forest, he knew that Kali was taking its revenge and he seemed powerless. But...but was he? Caught between two terrible propositions, he regained his courage, a measure of it. Not for once did he seriously contemplate returning to the clearing in the forest – assuming he could find it. Dare the forest again? Nah!

He picked himself up and, clutching his briefcase, began to walk toward the village square. Did he not know his politics? Had he not played with the Bante Lams and the J. I. D. Asalams? Did the elders think he was sold on that story that the village no longer traded with money when they were probably waiting for him to drop dead before pouncing on his briefcase? Could Kali have lost its material hunger when all the evidence around him – the graveyard, the elders, the forest, the road proclaimed otherwise? *I will not die, Kali, and you too will not die. That is the new covenant that I have come to make. That is the new covenant that we will make. Together, Kali, together!*

"Today, I stand before you, Kali, naked in truth," he began when he at last stood in the village square, surrounded by silent, expressionless faces. "Naked in the truth that Kali and I are one, naked in the truth that, together, we can accomplish all things. Should the past overtake us? Should we be ransomed by the past? Today, I have come to make a new covenant with you."

He opened his briefcase and began to shower his audience with currency notes. But not a muscle stirred, not an expression changed. A voice within him counseled a new direction, so he began another speech.

"Mr. Speaker sir, without bothering to seek your permission, I will tell you that you and everyone else in this so-called House of the People is a hyenarable farthead – a skunk with a cloud of fart for a brain. How many times did I stand on the floor of this accursed House and plead and thunder and state and query and argue and cite and...and thunder that my people were dying? How many many times? It gives me great pleasure, therefore, to move and to second and to pass and to sign that this House of Bandits be disbanded forthwith so that my people, our people, so that we will breathe again. Dust to dust, ashes to ashes."

Uduak sensed it even before he heard it – the funereal beats of the Death Drum. It was like a long-awaited signal. His audience transformed into a howling mass as they set on him. The onslaught did not cease until Ime Uduak, Honorable Member of Parliament, lay lifeless in the center of the pile of currency notes that was, in his reckoning, the blood of a new covenant.

"You are dead. And Kali has buried you," pronounced one of the five gaunt, old men.

When Ime Uduak, Honorable Member of Parliament, awoke, he knew that – to him and his new covenant – the village had vanished, perhaps forever. But his nightmare remained – how to placate the forest, how to accomplish a resurrection.

—

1995

Printed by Libri Plureos GmbH in Hamburg, Germany